PÁLAVA
PUBLISHING

CZECH FICTION SERIES

MICHAL VIEWEGH

DODGEBALL

MICHAL VIEWEGH

DODGEBALL

translated by
David Short

PÁLAVA PUBLISHING
BRNO 2018

Originally published in Czech as Vybíjená in 2015

© Michal Viewegh, 2004, 2015
© Druhé město—Martin Reiner, 2015
Translation © David Short, 2018
© Pálava Publishing, 2018

PAVLOVSKÝ s.r.o.
Published in co-operation with Dana Blatná Literary Agency

Cover art by Jan Pražan
Cover photo by Euromedia Group, a.s.
Cover and book design by Bedřich Vémola

ISBN 978-80-906428-9-8

www.palavapublishing.com

This translation was made possible by a grant from the Ministry of Culture of the Czech Republic.

MINISTRY OF CULTURE
CZECH REPUBLIC

TOM

When you're twenty, flat-sharing with two others of the same age can be quite fun; at forty-one it ceases to be a joke.

Occasionally, you might be woken by thirst and the makings of a hangover, so you get up for a drink of chlorinated tap-water, since there's no point looking for a bottle of *your own* beer or mineral water in the fridge. You're too lazy to find your slippers in the dark, so your gloomy expectation of feeling prickly dried breadcrumbs, paprika-flavoured crisps, Skippy's nail clippings, squashed olives pickled in garlic vinegar and God knows what else under your bare feet is fulfilled. Then you skid on some Eurotel brochures left lying around. Skippy gets a new mobile three times a year, changes his payment plan every month and never stops counting how many free minutes he's got left despite having next to no one to phone. And I'm no better—we've both got more free minutes than we know what to do with. You can hear your flatmates in *No. 1* and *No. 3* snoring away, and on the cork notice-board in the hall you can make out the faint glimmer of the sheet of A4 with your latest vain attempt at setting up a monthly flat-cleaning rota. You silently open the bathroom door, grope for the rubber vagina with which

7

Skippy replaced the light switch one wet weekend two years ago, you pinch its lips together and the light comes on. Then you slowly open your eyes: you see the three razors lying on the unbelievably filthy washbasin. The mirror above is spattered with so many kinds of toothpaste that it puts you in mind of a less than successful abstract painting. You turn on the tap, let it run and gaze at your wrinkled forehead and baggy eyes. You listen to the water streaming down the plughole: in the silence of the flat at night the sound strikes you as oddly more meaningful than in the daytime. As if it carries some coded message—a message for you: *Not so good, is it, pal? And it's gonna get worse.*

You aren't even very surprised. You might even nod in agreement, turn the tap off and haul yourself back to bed. Your own bed. In *No. 2.*

EVA

Now she's divorced she'll stay single.

They'd all told her that at twenty-nine and with her physiognomy (how she hates that word) she'd have no problem finding a bloke, but she isn't actually looking for one. She might accept the odd invitation for coffee or the theatre—but nothing ever comes of it. Mostly she senses from the outset that it's sort of... a struggle. The men all try so hard, and that's probably where it all goes wrong. She smiles, notes their expensive ties and listens to one witty story after another (Jeff used to insist that her lack of a sense of humour bordered on a mental handicap), but inside she can't wait to get back home, run a bath with mandarin-scented foam and listen to her new U2 CD. Does any of this make sense? Most of her friends (not to mention her mother) would say that it doesn't.

But she can't help herself. Her very beauty seems to debilitate men in advance. She uses the expression *beauty* in the same matter-of-fact way as rich people talk about money—to the less well-endowed it obviously sounds snooty. But it isn't really. She isn't snooty and she finds compliments more or less irksome. 'Why the hell does this guy go on as if he's just discovered America?' Okay, she's beautiful, and she knows it—so what then?

She's not sure she can explain it. Many of the men who've danced attendance on her since the divorce go in for all kinds of romantic gestures: giving her diamond rings that she returns with an apology; buying plane tickets to London, which they then have to cancel at some considerable cost; laying their entire lives (sometimes including the wife and children) at her feet. They pretend to be ready to burn all their bridges—apparently believing that she's only to be won over by whoever makes the greatest sacrifice. Sometimes she feels like a luxury apartment—first refusal to the highest bidder.

Everything is so predictable. At first they're all bubbling over with confidence, but once they see there's no change in her reserve, the bubble bursts. They start treating her the way they would a boss and begin to be afraid of her. They keep asking if she's enjoying the meal, if she needs anything or if there's anything they can do for her. They'll do anything. They might even go down on one knee. How can she be impressed by men like that? It's so tiresome. So ridiculous. Skippy probably put it best one time: "We're all shit-scared of you." She'd never have put it like that herself (vulgarity isn't her thing), but there was some truth in it. Can it really be that there's no one who isn't... shit-scared of her?

Her idea of things is quite different. "You've got no bloody idea," Jeff shouted at her one time before their divorce, beside himself with rage. Sometimes she has this weird dream: someone rings the bell and she goes to the door in her dressing-gown. Outside there's a stranger, who greets her with his eyes only. She stands aside, the man enters and starts helping her pack; she opens her wardrobe, takes out the hangers and he folds the clothes away into suitcases. Neither of them speaks the whole time. Her daughter Alice eyes her enquiringly, but she indicates by a look that it's all okay. The man closes the suitcases, picks up the larger one and takes Alice by the hand. She takes the other case. Unhurriedly, they go down to the waiting car and the man drives her to his house...

It's so hard to explain everything. It's all about communication, Jeff used to say.

"Communicate with me. Talk to me. How can I begin to understand those mysterious feminine feelings if you won't even try to describe them? How the hell can I make sense of you?"

Alice complains that she's taken to spending more and more time in the bathroom. She could be right at that; she hasn't been keeping check herself. Now she's passed forty, the list of cosmetic defects that need treating, or at least concealing, every morning is growing at such a rate that it's begun to make her uneasy. At eighteen she needed barely five minutes in the bathroom: she would clean her teeth, dash some cold water on her face, apply the first cream that came to hand, run a brush through her hair—then all day long people would keep saying how beautiful she was. On Saturdays, when she came down to breakfast with the family, her father's face would beam with surprise, almost awe. To the extent that she felt it was a bit tactless with respect to her mother. Sometimes he even set down the newspaper he was reading, preferring to watch her as she tried to assemble the food processor in order to make some fresh juice out of three greeny-yellow Cuban oranges.

"You know, Alena, I can hardly believe we could conceive something *so* pretty in that scruffy bungalow on the Jugoslav Riviera," he said.

He would get up, gently push his daughter aside and assemble the juicer for her.

"I don't get it either," Eva's mother replied with a smile.

"It wasn't scruffy at all," she whispered to Eva. "Your dad's just making it up..."

It seems like only yesterday. Nowadays she spends an hour in the bathroom, and when she does reach the kitchen Alice tells her she should get her teeth whitened and treat the bags under her eyes with a green tea-bag.

"And if you're really not going to do anything about your hair, you should wear a headscarf."

Sometimes she thinks her daughter is starting to talk like Tom.

Most evenings she stays in. She used to go to a beginners' yoga class, but gave up after six months. She found the positions comical, and it cost her some effort to keep her amusement concealed from their enthusiastic trainer.

Paradoxically, she finally lost interest the moment she got the hang of the trickiest exercises. She was better at them than the others; the teacher would praise her and hold her up as an example, but she never ceased to find the unnatural postures embarrassing. 'So what if I can stand on my head, I'm still going to be just some divorcee,' she would ruminate.

She likes crosswords, knitting and watching a lot of television, whatever anyone else might think. In preference to films she likes documentaries, especially travel programmes. There's one in particular that she hardly ever misses. She's never been a great tourist and, truth to tell, she has no particular desire to travel ('What particular desires do I have left?' she's apt to ask herself), but now and again she does find herself wondering what life might have been like if she'd been born in some quite different country. If she'd gone to a girls' high school in Yemen, say.

"Yemen? You must be crazy, mum," Alice laughs at her. "Where on earth did you get that idea?"

Eva doesn't know. Is it her fault?

Television has filled her head with all manner of advertising slogans and jingles. Obviously, she hasn't meant to memorise that kind of stuff. It's just verbal ballast that she can't shed. Last week, on one of the squares nearby, she spotted a man peeing in the arcade. *Complete Savages* flashed through her mind. She redirected her gaze towards the roof of the nearest house. *Bramac. A Roof for Life.* She sometimes wonders if this isn't the onset of the menopause.

She travels to work by metro: during the morning rush it would take her almost twice as long if she took the car. The carriages are usually packed, which she heartily dislikes. If, on rare occasions, she does find a seat, she leafs through a newspaper. She only reads the back sections: Leisure, Culture, Health, Money; on the home and foreign news pages she just skims the headlines. She's never managed to cultivate any interest in politics. Being ruled more by instinct, she registers only what this or that politician looks, speaks or dresses like.

"You don't vote for parties, or manifestos," Jeff accused her the night before the general election, "you vote for suits! Ties!"

"Not just that," she protested weakly; she knew she couldn't win this one. "I also go by their eyes, their smiles, and things..."

"So if Grebeníček looked like Richard Gere, you'd vote Communist, would you?"

Sometimes she can't focus on her paper at all and instead watches the other passengers—especially the women. Through her feet she can feel the tons of steel undercarriage jolting and vibrating. 'How do you cope?' she sometimes wants to ask them. 'Don't you find life unbearably hard? How come we're still here? How come we haven't ended up like Irena, down there on the rails?'

TOM

At sixty-two, Vartecký is still looking good; from spring to autumn he cycles to school, he plays volleyball twice a week, and every Friday he takes his wife, sixteen years his junior, to the sauna. Some of the women teachers (and they are in a majority of 80% plus) go out of their way to make up to him, but he remains gloomily, but graciously unfazed. At parties like this one he's more akin to a big, gentle dog being bothered by children: he puts up with all the stroking, kissing and sitting on his lap with impressive forbearance, and only when such signs of affection hit the limits of what's tolerable does he get up, carefully disengage his tipsy colleague and saunter off to a far corner of the staffroom. I fetch him a chair, we clink glasses and chat about this and that. Mrs Mrázová comes past; with both hands she's clutching a paper tray bearing nothing but the greasy stain of two open sandwiches, a bit of gristle and a yellow arc of lemon peel. I lean slightly closer to Vartecký.

"And now the young hostesses are bringing the teachers of the year their well-deserved awards," I whisper.

Mrs Mrázová turns, measures us with her piercing eyes, then stretches her mouth into a smile that she presumably thinks is a bit saucy; a piece of egg yolk is trapped in her denture. 'She really ought to give up on saucy smiles,' I muse. She'd do better to pack them away in some musty old box on top of the wardrobe she stows her summer clothes in come October.

"Lovely party, eh?" I observe to be sociable.

Twenty-five years ago we didn't get on, but now we both do our best to disguise the fact. In those days she taught us maths and descriptive geometry. At one end-of-year test at the blackboard she had watched with unconcealed scorn as I struggled with some kind of *projection of a pyramid*.

"But Thomas, I thought you had some imagination—being the *poet* you are...," she'd said spitefully.

"I do have imagination, just no sense of space," I replied. "They're two quite different things, Miss."

My impertinence had left her dumbfounded. Does she still remember? In her time she's had hundreds of such rebels—I wonder if the numbers don't take the edge off their glory. Inflation of rebellion. I recall the comic rituality with which she used to wield her large wooden compasses, and can't suppress a smile.

"Have you two got some secret?" she asks suspiciously.

Vartecký looks at me.

"Actually we have," he says. "We both used to love the same girl."

Mrs Mrázová sighs disapprovingly:

"Can't you men ever talk about anything else?"

About an hour later, having run into Vartecký again, I go back to what he'd been hinting at—though I obviously wait for the right moment so the change of subject isn't too abrupt.

"One personal question about your past—may I?"

Vartecký has never been one to waste words, perhaps as a reaction against his garrulous lady colleagues—and, when talking to him, I've gradually adopted the same approach. He nods without hesitation.

"Did you have sex with her that time at Slapy?"

He doesn't need to ask who I mean, nor does he pretend to be trying to remember. I appreciate that, but at the same time it makes me uneasy: over the years he's taught dozens, if not hundreds of pretty girls.

"No."

He doesn't seem to be lying, but I'm not quite sure.

"And before then, or later?"

"No."

"Why not?" I ask in my blasé way.

His unbuttoned shirt reveals dense, only lightly greying hairs—my own chest is, by contrast, almost smooth, which is why, in his company, I usually adopt the posture of the ironising intellectual who despises that front-line mark of masculinity.

"When she came into my orchard / blossom time was nearly o'er. / Like some graceless vagabond / then the sun did sleepy soar..."

Escaping into poetry, I thought at once.

"Your wife's forty-six," I object. "When you married her she was only a couple of years older than Eva."

"Except she wasn't a pupil. It's not worth it with pupils. The pleasure is far outweighed by the problems."

I wait, but no further explanation is forthcoming.

"You ought to know something about that yourself," he merely adds, referring to Klára.

I still don't quite believe him, but I'm not cross at him: he's no reason to lie to me, so if he's not being frank about that business twenty years ago, he's just trying to show some consideration. He knows that for me the past isn't over.

"And did *you*?" he asks unexpectedly.

"Bingo!" I exclaim. "The key question. The nub of the matter."

"So you didn't have sex with her either?"

"No."

He says nothing.

"No. Just two little letters, N and O—and there's half a lifetime in them," I say.

The wine in plastic bottles isn't up to much, but I toss a whole glass down my throat anyway. Then I pour us a new glass each.

"But why not?" he enquires casually.

When I'd asked the same question there'd been a tremor in my voice. There's the difference, I realise: Jeff and I used to flutter excitedly around Eva, while he stood quietly by. We would wheel and turn about her, never stop talking, sometimes reciting poems—he said nothing. We would avert our eyes, while his gaze was direct and uninhibited. I suspected it even back then: how could she be impressed by someone who was paralysed by her beauty? She needed someone who could simply take that beauty to himself. Outwardly, Jeff and I would make fun of Vartecký's age (may we be forgiven!), whereas in reality we were scared of him. We were acutely aware that he'd got something that we, with the best will in the world, could never have.

"How would I know?" I exclaim. "Because you were there. Because she'd become Jeff's girlfriend. Whatever."

Vartecký placed a finger on his lips. Marta, once my PE teacher, turned towards us with an amused glint in her eye.

"Aha, so we're back to Eva Šálková, eh?"

Vartecký adopts a phlegmatic expression, I maintain a stony silence like a boy caught scrumping (teaching at the school you once attended as a pupil is an odd perversion—it's tempting to say that it's almost incestuous. In the past I attributed returning to my alma mater as a teacher to a healthy conservatism or sentimentality; today I realise that it was due in part to social inertia: I simply couldn't be bothered to look for a life other than the one I knew so well). Marta shook her head in disbelief.

"Šálková *forever!*" she laughs at her own English.

"Spot on, Marta," I reply earnestly. "Šálková forever."

EVA

She does drive, but only on the two routes she knows by heart: the Friday shopping trip to the Hypernova supermarket, and once a fortnight to see her parents in Vrchlabí; after retiring they'd sold their Prague flat and bought a little house there. Otherwise she takes the car nowhere. Her burgundy Renault stands in the same spot for days on end (in winter it is often the only car in the street covered in snow, and in summer, when she leaves it nearer the park, it only takes a week and it's usually covered by a thick dusting of yellow pollen in which the local kids draw dirty pictures). She'd been given it last year—seven years after their divorce—as a birthday present from Jeff.

"What are you after?" she'd asked him.

"Only that the pair of you'll survive."

It is said to be the safest car in its class.

She knows the route to Vrchlabí by heart, every road sign, every bend; whenever, like right now, she has to switch to a different lane from the one she's used to being in she's immediately thrown off-balance.

"Mummy?" Alice is about to tease her: "What would you do the day they put in a thirty-kilometre diversion at this spot?"

Obviously, the possibility has occurred to her too. She watches the rear wheels of the Ford in front. *Sixty per cent more siping than on other brands of tyre*, she recalls and gets annoyed with herself.

"I'd pull over, switch my hazard lights on and phone for a tow."

She glances briefly at her daughter: something about the girl's smile gives her an almost painful reminder of Jeff that first time she saw him. He wasn't quite sixteen and a centimetre shorter than her. Since then, though, he'd rapidly outgrown her in every respect.

As she's parking the car in the yard behind the house she spots her father standing behind the curtain—he doesn't pull it back, as if there's some reason for him to put off the moment of coming out to greet them. As if he needs two or three minutes to think something over. 'Return of the prodigal only child,' Eva thinks.

"You're our everything. Our pride and joy. Don't you ever forget that." That's what her mother always used to say.

Obviously, that's not the sort of thing you say about daughters who've reached forty. She'd love to believe she still is their everything, or almost everything, though they haven't said as much for years. Perhaps because this *almost everything* has suddenly taken on the aspect of an aging divorcee with a child. She understands she's been a disappointment to them. They'd brought her up the best way they could. They'd sacrificed everything for her. She'd been literally pampered. Take just the endless expensive tanning creams and sun screens that they'd squandered on her every year at those Adriatic coastal resorts... And how's she repaid them? She's got divorced, and to crown it all her age is starting to show. 'Sorry, Daddy, your pretty little girl has got varicose veins...' She takes a deep breath. As ever, the air is so much cleaner, crisper than in Prague. Just beyond the garage roof she can see the grey-green slopes of Žalý Ridge. Her father comes out—in his tracksuit, which briefly hurts her. Her mother follows him out, carrying a steaming saucepan that she sets down on the steps. 'For sixty years they lived in a fairly decent part of Prague—and now this,' she muses.

"Hiya!" she calls, making an effort.

Alice runs to her grandma and hugs her. Grandma smiles, but her eyes are on the saucepan.

"Gimme the keys, let me straighten it up," her father says.

She hands him the keys blankly; only now does she see that the car is standing at a bit of an odd angle, with half of one front tyre resting on the low sandstone edging round a bed of dahlias. Flowers for All Souls. *Flowers for every occasion.* Her father struggles to get behind the steering wheel, eases the seat back, turns the ignition and listens to the engine; then he puts it in reverse and in two simple moves has the car straightened up. He doesn't get out yet and lowers the window.

"Pretty good car," he says.

"Jeff was here yesterday," her mother informs her.

She says nothing.

"You need a few more practice drives," her father remarks as he gets back out.

"If you say so. Thanks for the warm welcome."

He makes a dismissive gesture with one hand, then puts an arm around her.

"Hi," he says finally with a smile.

When she was living with Jeff, he did nearly all the driving; like many other married men he would only let her drive when he'd been drinking. She hated driving when he was drunk. Given her lack of experience, she needed him to navigate and give her instructions, but either he treated her nervous questions (Which way now? Quick! Who's got right of way? Me, or that truck?) with all the casual indifference of a drunkard, or he'd lose his cool and start snapping at her.

After the divorce, she decided one evening, while she was having a bath, to break out of the magic circle of just two familiar routes: she would go round to the nearest driving school, book half a dozen, or, better, a dozen, practice lessons, and learn to drive anywhere, not just to Vrchlabí. She had visions of going on day-trips with Alice at the weekend.

"How long have you had a licence?" was the first thing the instructor asked.

They were already in the car.

"Twenty years, but until I got divorced my husband did all the driving."

The instructor looked her over.

"Not another divorcee," he muttered. "Start the engine."

Eva couldn't strike the right response to his rudeness; her mind was focussed on the unfamiliar layout of the dashboard.

"Let's go then. What are you waiting for?"

The instructor's bearishness reminded her of something all too familiar. At the very next lights she looked straight into his ruddy features—and it hit her.

"You've been drinking," she said, awestruck.

The instructor laughed in such a way as to kill off any lingering doubts she might have had. She switched on the hazard lights, pulled on the handbrake and undid her seat-belt.

"I'm not going any further," she told him. "You're pissed!"

"I am most certainly not pissed."

"You are."

She got out and left. People were watching her. The cars behind started tooting their horns.

"And you're just like all other non-drinkers: boring, exasperating and a cold fish!" the instructor shouted after her.

JEFF

He's never really been able to fathom Eva out. That's the one sure thing that survives after all that's happened.

Whenever he tries to look at it rationally, it gets him nowhere—except to a sense that if he carries on along the same lines for a few minutes more he'll go mad. 'If you're thinking about women,' he sometimes tells Tom, 'you can forget anything that's rational. That road leads nowhere.' He can give him dozens of examples: Eva complains about the populism or lack of principle among Czech politicians, and when he asks her why, then, did she vote for the party whose chairman is the very quintessence of populism and lack of principle, she says it's because he's got 'that something', dresses well and has nice hands. And so on and so on. Whenever the subject arises, Jeff feels he's going to choke.

"Look, we live in a logically structured world: continents, countries, districts and so on down the line," he explains to Tom. "This is reflected in the relevant institutions. Whatever you think about contemporary society, there's no denying one thing: it has a clear hierarchy."

"Your meaning being?"

"I'm obviously not saying that all institutions work perfectly, but at least their structure is transparent: the organs of state, district councils, town halls. Pure logic. And now try and fit the family, the basic building block of society, into the system," Jeff laughs bitterly: "One half of it can't stick to logic even to discuss a Bruce Willis film... There must be a flaw somewhere, don't you think?"

Tom smiles.

"Take Klára," Jeff says. "What *is* marriage? You love her sincerely—and yet after every other sentence she utters you could up and kill her. *That's* marriage. That's why you run away from her. Why you play volleyball every Tuesday evening and indoor football on Thursdays. Why you go skiing at weekends. Why you'll buy a bike and any chance you get you'll head off somewhere just to get as far away from her as you can."

"I thought you went cycling together?"

Jeff shakes his head.

"The fact that I sometimes took her with me doesn't alter the principle of escape. When she was peddling away behind me in silence, it wasn't really her—if you know what I mean."

After a longish pause Tom nods.

"Basically it's to keep them from talking," Jeff adds gravely.

THE AUTHOR

At fourteen-and-a-half he measured 162 centimetres.

He liked wearing plain, open-necked shirts with a silk neck-tie. The brown suede jacket was made for him by his grandmother, Věra, a furrier. She was obviously pleased with her efforts: when the author put the jacket on for the first time, she used the word 'style' or 'stylish' several times over.

"You've got style, lad," she smiled.

The author sensed that his schoolmates made fun of him behind his back and that Grandma's assessment was somewhat over the top, but that word did have a certain allure for him. Suppose Grandma was right? What if what's so stylish about him partly rubbed off on the girls in his class? To play safe, he wore his jacket and shirts with a silk cravat right through his first year—with the obvious exception of national holidays, when, like the rest of the class, he had to don his Young Communist outfit of blue shirt and red tie.

Later on, one of his parents' friends gave him a green-and-white anorak of latex-coated paper, picked up from the Grundig stand at the Brno Trade Fair. It had a zip. Discounting the ladies' Levis that his mother sometimes lent him (until his last year at school he possessed no other genuine denim garment), that promotional anorak was the most modern, most *Western* item in his less-than-modest wardrobe. He wore it all through his second and third year. In the final weeks the arms were somewhat out-at-elbow and looked generally scruffy, but he wouldn't give up wearing it.

At the very beginning of the first year, the author followed the example of his two closest friends and refused to eat in the school canteen (Whose example were those two following? he wondered as he was writing these lines) and all three of them had their lunch at one of the two delicatessens in the town every day for four years. For four years, five days a week, they had slices of warm meatloaf or Italian salad, with two bread rolls in either case. From time to time they'd treat themselves to a pair of top-of-the-range frankfurters or even 'Russian' eggs. They drank lemonade or Kofola, Czechoslovakia's unique answer to Coke. They *never* ate or drank anything else—and they absolutely didn't mind. What's more, if the author's memory doesn't deceive him, they actually *enjoyed* it. Over the duration of their four years at high school, they are calculated to have had *meatloaf* four hundred times, *Italian salad* three hundred times, and the frankfurters or those dreadful eggs with their greeny-grey yolks a hundred times—and he'd never complained. With hindsight he doesn't understand how, and at the recollection of all those kilos of greasy meatloaf and those litres of mayonnaise he even has a delayed sense of being about to throw up, something akin to a metaphysical belch. Had it really been he? He, who these days can hold a generally informed discussion with the waiter in any Italian, Mexican, Chinese, Thai, Indian or Lebanese restaurant? He, who can barely stand any other fish than *sushi* or any other pasta than *home-made*? He, whose evening can be ruined if his crème brûlée comes without the caramelised topping or his tiramisu is made without genuine mascarpone?

To put it in terms of encyclopaedias of zoology: *When they are young, theirs is a simple diet; in later years they become highly selective.*

Is there a lesson in that? The author isn't sure.

In his third year, the PE teacher, somewhat surprisingly, nominated him for the school basketball team, which was about to enter some competition. He was the only one in the team who didn't play regularly; the other boys trained several times a week at the municipal sports club. They received him with a measure of distrust, but were soon persuaded that he deserved his place: his shooting might not have been the most accurate, but he was a half-decent defender and it wasn't unknown for him to capture the odd seemingly lost ball.

In the final match of the competition the opposition scored in the last minute, causing his side to lose by a single point. The overall standings were already decided (whatever the outcome of this match they'd be third out of six teams), but this dramatic conclusion had all the spectators and both benches on their feet. During a breakaway, one of his team members was attacked and, under pressure, made a fumbling pass to the author, but he managed to grab the ball at the last moment. "Shoot!" someone bellowed at him. "You must shoot!" The author dribbled niftily past the nearest opponent, jumped and scored the deciding basket—which he remembers to this day.

To this day he remembers his only basket from a trifling game in an insignificant tournament.

TOADY

To the point: I'm not pretty. Not a bit, seriously. I'm really *more plain than not*, which, unfortunately, is not false modesty, but the truth of the matter. Show my photo (perhaps the ghastly one from my ID card, or even the slightly better one in my passport, or the one on my driving licence—it makes little odds) to ten randomly selected people and offer them four options: *beautiful*, *quite pretty*, *more plain than not*, and *plain*—and you can bet your life that at least seven of them will instantly tick C, though any pubertal pipsqueak, no matter how bad his own acne, will obviously go for D.

So this is what I have to live with—except that it's not my mugshot that I exhibit to people in the street, but my real mug. Even to pubertal yobs.

My lack of looks is hard to describe: I don't have a hunchback, a monstrous nose or eyebrows that meet in the middle. It's not the product of any such conspicuous, and so relatively easily removed, single feature; no, it comes as the simple product of several dozen minor, at first sight insignificant, physical shortcomings: my face could be more oval, my forehead higher, my hair thicker, my eyes larger, my ears smaller, my gaze rather more penetrating, my teeth whiter and straighter, my complexion clearer and more radiant, my mouth better shaped, my lips fuller, my hips and bottom trimmer, my legs longer. And so on. There's so much wrong that with the best will in the world I can do nothing about it. As a certain architect said to a lady client who'd bought an ancient house somewhere beyond the outskirts of Prague: "There's so much needs doing that the best solution would be to knock it down and start from scratch..." That's me to a T: laser treatments, liposuction and plastic surgery will solve nothing. My best solution is *demolition*.

In short I'm the one they call Toady.

That's all I've been known as ever since primary school. Regrettably I can't remember whose idea it was first—if I did know, I'd run him down in my car (just joking!). It might have been Skippy, but I could be wrong.

Anyway, the name stuck. It sounds mocking enough and so it neatly encapsulates my then self: the permanent scowl, cheap specs, pubertal lip-hair and drooping shoulders. In a sense Toady is brilliant shorthand for the whole me.

Větvičková—Toady. My entire childhood is in those two names. Větvičková, her surname reduced rather unimaginatively to Větev, 'the Branch', or Twiglet as I preferred to think of her, is a mite worse off. In my *objective* view she's as ugly as sin—I'm not really that bad by comparison. We take the same tram to school. Imagine the scene: two unattractive girls standing alone in the morning mist by the tram-stop. Obviously, I'm wearing the smile that goes with my sense of superiority, firm in my belief that I can't possibly be as *ghastly* as Větvičková. Aesthetically she's *the pits*.

Except that as we enter Year Eight after the summer holidays a quite different Větvičková arrives: tanned, nice breasts, and with a remarkably fetching hairdo (as I register with a stab of envy the moment I spot her). Even now, she isn't much to write home about, but one thing is clear to all: the much-loved competition for the title of *Miss Classroom Ogress* is for once going to have a touch of drama. Will Twiglet defend her title—or will she lose out to Toady? In the event, I beat her by a whisker, but one lesson has stuck with me for the rest of my life: if I let the care of my appearance slip for a second, I will be the premier Ugly Duckling. (Incidentally, you might try imagining how, faced with this certain knowledge, you could ever *relax*... Is it any surprise, then, that I've always found the idea of *relaxing* somewhat ludicrous?)

For unprepossessing girls like me, beauty will sooner or later become the sole criterion in all things. Even at the age of three I would choose the place in the sandpit from where there was the nicest view. I *never* played among dustbins—not me! I would choose ice-cream for its *colour*—so it wouldn't clash too much with what I was wearing. Don't you see? A little girl in glasses and shapeless blue cords isn't going to buy a pistachio ice-cream even if she fancies one, because she's afraid of the colour contrast... Blue and green must never be seen. Can you envisage the tribulation of a charmless twelve-year-old who can't afford *yet another* failing?

At high school I gave every appearance of sharing the same values as my classmates, but deep inside I knew it was all claptrap. Friendship? Selflessness? Fairness? Truth?—Rubbish! The only thing that really matters in the life of a woman is looks. The *simple truth* is that selfless, friendly or fair-minded girls do not become recipients of love-letters.

I secretly watched them in class—my prettier classmates. Every morning I tried to guess what they would turn up in, fearful of the invisible aura that often accompanied their arrival. That aura might well have been invisible to the rest, but I could see it—and I bet Twiglet could as well. Incredibly, the silly geese looked fantastic, no matter how ungainly their walk or untidy their appearance. Bleary-eyed, hair all squashed, T-shirts crumpled, even with a grimy head-band—paradoxically, all it did was enhance their charm. Their eyes stood out the more, their complexion seemed even smoother.

To this day I remember every detail of their clothes. Don't you see? After twenty-five years I still have the clearest image of the Wild Cat denim skirt on Eva Šálková when she came into the classroom in our second year: every pocket, every slit, even the red-and-blue label.

In class I never stopped spying on her. During art lessons she would stick her tongue half out and I kept trying to figure why she looked so tremendously sexy even with her tongue out. If I stuck mine out I'd look like a mental case (though fortunately I had enough good sense never to do it).

"Oh God," I whispered to myself, "why is it okay for her and not for me?"

I grew into a rabid atheist, and all because God hadn't endowed me with a better mug. From puberty on I never entered any kind of church—just as I never go back to any restaurant where I've been cheated.

Frequently during adolescence it occurred to me that if I didn't have such big breasts and bum I could pretend to be sort of independent. *Love? Sex? No thanks, not interested.* But with a D-cup? With the arse of a prize-winning Cuban mother I'd never convince anyone I wasn't made for love. Anyone could see I was—but as soon as they looked into my face they could tell at once that I was desperately short of it.

I'm not independent, I'm just plain ugly. I can't fool anyone.

I'm forty, yet I'm still measuring everything mostly in terms of *allure*—not just, shall we say, cars or mobile phones (obviously what matters most is an elegant shape and the colour, not the technology inside), but neighbours as well, or doctors, or politicians. What use are beautiful visions to a politician if he's got a crooked smile and a triple chin? I certainly wouldn't vote for him. And anyway: I've only ever liked good-looking, or at least pleasant guys. You see the magnitude of this catastrophe? Me, so plain as I am, and *only* drawn to blokes with charm.

You try living with this fatal combination—and surviving.

EVA

Working as a solicitor for a foreign company may at first sight seem quite tricky, but in fact it's just as primitive as one of those word-search games: always the same words, the same phrases. And there are more similarities: leaving aside the salary, she would say that the job is about as much use to her in life as doing crosswords: a moderately sophisticated way of killing time.

She is considered able, even successful, though she's never found it especially difficult: all you needed was good English, a measure of commitment, an ability to communicate with others and knowing how to prioritise the various tasks at hand. She still enjoys the work, though she's long been aware that her job and real life are worlds apart. When, at a lunch, she meets all those perfectly groomed, self-confident young men in their Hugo Boss suits, she remembers Jeff back in the early nineties: he also believed that the job he'd just landed was his great chance in life. She hears them ordering (two of the *veal saltimbocca*, one *spaghetti vongole* and one *pasta al ragù di coniglio*) and, laughing, she sees them toss their jackets over their chairs and watches them chewing—and she thinks of Jeff. Sometimes she remembers Karel as well, and Irena. She's never guessed how much space in her head would be filled with dead people who hadn't struck her as particularly important when they were alive. She can even remember the exact dates when they died; those two years have become part of her own history for all eternity—much like her parents' wedding-day or the birth of her daughter. But then she's not alone: when, at a class reunion, she says, none too happily, that Alice was born *two years after Karel*, most of her classmates know at once what she means.

From the very start of their marriage Jeff used to come in from work quite late, generally when Alice was already asleep. He'd usually be tired and irritable. She understood, he was having a hard time of it: as ever, he wanted to be a winner, but the terms of this race were far from fair.

"How can I compete with people who can afford to buy whole factories for cash?" he said, getting quite het up.

She would have loved to talk to him, since she herself had hardly exchanged a word all day with another adult, but he wouldn't open up, keeping to the shortest of sentences. He roamed the apartment saying nothing, bent down with a groan and ostentatiously picked up the scattered toys.

"This isn't a home, it's a battlefield."

"She went on playing after kids' television finished," Eva explained, trying to be conciliatory. "I tidy up after her five times a day as it is."

"In which case it looks as if you'll have to do it six times."

"Not likely! You can tidy up."

Verbal dodgeball. Two captains.

"I've been slogging my guts out all day at work."

"Do you suppose I've been sitting around doing nothing?"

They both sensed how deep they'd sunk. Jeff collapsed into an armchair and rubbed the bridge of his nose.

"I can't stand mess," he said quietly. "Can't you grasp that?"

Jeff tried to make up for his weekday absence at the weekend. Alice still wasn't quite two, but he was already planning long days out walking.

"That's crazy," Eva protested as they craned over the map. "No child could walk that far."

"Mine can," Jeff insisted.

Then, of course, for most of the way Alice had to be carried, at which they took turns.

The pair of them were forever holding Jeff back.

"Please, love, can't you hurry up a bit?" he tended to say fractiously whenever Eva was getting Alice dressed.

"Of course I can," Eva smiled back bravely. "That is, if you don't mind that it's minus two outside and she won't have either a jumper or her anorak."

When they were out walking, the girls would *dawdle*. Jeff was always a few yards ahead and kept looking back reproachfully.

"She's a *baby*, Jeff," Eva reminded him tetchily. "You can't ask for miracles."

"I'm not asking for miracles. I just want you to get a move on!"

And when they went out for a bike ride, they *lagged behind*.

"For Christ's sake, step on it, will you?" Jeff would call back before riding in furious circles round and round them.

"We can't, idiot!" Eva shouted back.

Jeff couldn't take it any more and made a break for it: he bore down on his pedals and within three seconds was out of sight round the next bend.

"Where's Daddy gone?" Alice asked, worried; she had a fine sense for any tension in the air.

"Ahead."

An hour later Jeff would reappear, coming towards them: hunched over the handlebars, covered in mud, sweating and content.

"You ride your bike beautifully," he would praise Alice. "I'm so pleased with you."

SKIPPY

Did you know that daddy penguins spend six months keeping their eggs warm with their own bodies while the mummies are away goodness knows where for that entire time? For six months the males *stand there* in the freezing cold and the wind. There's this one huge flock of them, slowly shifting their feet and working round in spirals so that the ones at the edge always get a brief turn in the middle, where I assume it's less windy. I've no idea how they do it, but the egg is always at thirty-seven degrees, wherever they're standing. And whenever the little guy inside wants something, he just squeaks to his dad through the shell. Then the mother comes back from her six-month gallivant and takes the egg over. She can recognise her chick by its squeak. I know it's no big deal really, but I find it interesting. At any rate, it's a damn sight more interesting than what I'm reading here in the paper, that 2004 will be the year of Putin and Bush. A KGB man and a man who favours the death penalty... At airports these days they want your fingerprints (mind you, I reckon it's not for the prints themselves, but so they can tell whether you wipe your arse with your left hand like the Arabs, tee-hee), but when you get on a plane two or three years from now they'll implant your boarding pass under your skin at the back of your neck. And when you go to take a leak on the plane, there'll be at least four people in the Pentagon deciphering the sound. So that's the world we're living in, in case you're in any doubt. And you also shouldn't be in any doubt that I couldn't care less about politics. Not that I ever could. I've never been able to live a lie. It's true I was the only one in my class who refused to join the Union of Socialist Youth, but why the hell treat that as politics, like our class teacher did? At fifteen? Are you mad, Miss? It was only later that it dawned on me that she was also chair of the school's Party organisation. She couldn't make me change and she never took her eyes off me. Long after the Fifteenth Party Congress, she would make a point of checking my ID card in person just to see whether I hadn't made a tear on page 15 as a token protest—but that just wouldn't have occurred to me. A bit of attention, that's all I was after. Not joining the USY was basically no different from pricking my face with a safety-pin or biting worms in half when I was at primary school. The girls would squeal 'Ugh!' and pretend to be going to throw up, but it was better than nothing. I'd caught their attention—and that's always been the thing, hasn't it? You need to stand out from the crowd, otherwise no one's going to take a blind bit of notice of you. So in the first year at high school, when our Russian teacher handed out the addresses of some Russian kids and wanted us to be nice and friendly and write to them for a year, I told her I'd rather write to someone in Australia. Goodness, why Australia of all places? Because I've always liked kangaroos. She huffed and puffed and said she'd have to speak to the headmaster, but I reckon I carried it off pretty well. Fuck Vladivostok—Melbourne! Kindly ignore any swear-words; for me they're like politics, they mean bugger all.

TOADY

The facts: I was born on the twenty-second of November nineteen hundred and sixty-two—one year to the day before they shot John F. Kennedy (I sometimes wonder whether that assassination didn't foreshadow all those other premature deaths...)—to a thirty-five-year-old divorced bus driver and a seventeen-year-old commercial college student.

For years I wasn't the slightest bit interested in my mother; most of what I know about her I only learned from my father last year, and this year in hospital. If you've had any experience of regularly visiting people described as chronically sick, then you'll know how the time drags for those of us who are well. Let's not pretend: after six months, if not before, our reserves of compassion and understanding have been largely exhausted and the warehouse of our heart begins to reveal the bare walls of duty and boredom (sometimes I catch myself speaking like Tom). Dad and I have been over every conceivable topic umpteen times, so that in recent weeks we've mostly said nothing, just staring at the blue stripes on the hospital bedding and exchanging the odd encouraging smile. Once a minute the clock on the white wall gives out a dry click. I think hard of what else to tell him—but what is there to tell someone who probably won't be there in a couple of months' time? Try talking to a dying man about the problems of finding a place to park or the latest trends in Scandinavian furniture... From the start, awareness of this had me paralysed, so after a few weeks I was glad to latch on to any topic of conversation that was more or less *fit for purpose*—even one that was quite recently still taboo in our one-parent household.

"I've never known this, but where did you actually meet?" I asked him casually, though in reality the question was loaded with a perverse, masochistic excitement. "You and my *mother*, I mean?" I added with some irony.

At first my father looked surprised—and then he pulled a wry face. So this is all that's going to be left, I told myself: one wry look. I was reminded again of how the approach of death reduces proportions. A family drama of many years was suddenly just a silly story. Dad's lips were dry, so I gave him a drink of mineral water with a hint of orange. I felt sure he was more focussed on the plastic bottle than my question.

"I was asking where you met."

"On my bus," he said. "Where else?"

They took his bus to school five times a week—*that whole group*. In the morning, and again in the afternoon. For several months *two* of the girls had flirted with him. On the day in question *she in particular* had been playing up so badly that he nearly threw her off the bus.

"Exactly what you should have done," I couldn't stop myself saying. "Preferably while it was moving."

Briefly he looked slightly outraged, but then despite his progressive mental degradation he must have realised that rebukes of the order *That's no way to speak of your mother!* would sound pretty absurd in our case. He smiled a tooth-less smile—it didn't put me off, I was used to the sight.

"Yeah, perhaps I should've."

I kept on with my questions and from Dad's terse answers built up a mosaic of that February afternoon: after school, the two girls stayed on his bus all the way to the terminus, where they refused to alight. They offered him a cigarette as a sop. He took it. After all, he had a forty-minute lie-over. The taller one was the prettier of the two, but she had to go and buy *her mother some distilled water before they closed.*

I couldn't believe what I was hearing.

"Hang on," I gasped. "So if the mother of the taller girl hadn't run out of *distilled water*, she could have been my grandma?"

It was a while before he grasped it. Then he laughed and repeated my little joke several times over; at the same time he looked round to see if the other patients had heard him, but fortunately they were both asleep. It crossed my mind that if only the chemist's had closed an hour later, I might possibly have been beautiful.

He watched me and apparently remembered what I do for a living, for which he was proud of me—but because of which he also liked to take the mickey.

"So, have the Danes got round to inventing a five-legged chair yet?"

I shook my head with a smile, but I was thinking about my mother. That year she'd be fifty-seven.

"And Daddy?" I winked at him. "Did you make me that very first time. During that lie-over?"

He shifted his hand on the bedcover, as if meaning to flap my question away—so I knew I'd guessed right.

"And in the depot, or inside the bus?" I asked *teasingly*.

"You can't expect me to tell *you* things like that!"

He backed up his refusal with a sigh, but I could tell from his expression that he'd tell me in the end. Ultimately this wasn't one of those topics that had worn thin, so it stirred his lukewarm interest—though I did worry that his interest had been sparked less by my conception than by the word *bus*. He was silent. Apparently reminiscing.

"Inside the bus?"

He nodded, grabbed the trapeze bar and lumberingly made to sit up; he signalled that discussion of my conception was at an end.

"Where exactly?" I persisted.

"At the back!" he growled, dying to be free of my questions. "Where there's four seats together!"

So that's the secret of my coming into being: in a bus, *on the four seats at the rear*!

TOM

Jeff's oldest surviving photo from his high-school days, obviously black-and-white, was taken on a skiing course in year one, when we were fourteen: fair hair reaching (like mine in those days) the limit of what the times would tolerate, the comical hint of a moustache and that customary quizzical expression in his lovely eyes. Things missing from the picture include the inevitable lolloping walk that would keep breaking into a run, his habit of tipping his head to one side as he talked, and the short, deep furrow that would appear between his eyebrows whenever he disagreed with something.

My friendship with Jeff, which goes back over a quarter of a century, began during that lesson in September when the geography mistress was showing us something or other on the overhead projector—can't remember what it was, but I do remember that after the projection was over, the blind on one of the windows at the back of the classroom jammed. Jeff, who sat at a desk beneath the window, shot up (his chair screeched horribly) and, unbidden, took a short run and leapt up among the flowerpots on the marble window-sill. He tottered slightly—the class shrieked—but then, his balance immediately restored and using both hands, he pulled the blind back up. Then he jumped down, bowed and went back to his seat.

For a fraction of a second the class seemed uncertain as to what to make of his performance: should they approve of it as a clever bit of misconduct and a worthy display of gymnastics, or should they incline towards the attitude of the teacher, who had sarcastically tapped her forehead, and laugh at him, given that the entire sequence had something undeniably apelike about it.

"Nice one!" I shouted (the particular intonation that goes with this expression of approval, which as boys we used very often—and which, incidentally, I use to this day, for instance when Skippy and I are watching football, is achieved by letting it out sharply and in a deeper than normal voice; it usually helps if you wear a frown at the same time).

Jeff grinned at me and waved his appreciation. Thus it was that our friendship was launched by a dusty blind that had jammed.

During the very next break, in the corridor between classes, he came up to me.

"What have we got next?" he asked.

I reckon he knew.

"Maths."

I was glad he'd spoken to me and hurriedly tried to think of something to add to my reply so that it didn't sound so terse—but at that moment we were stopped by two final-year boys.

"Halt!" they commanded.

One of them was wearing glasses, and the other one wasn't particularly fearsome-looking either, but they were both a good few inches taller. We dutifully stopped. I recall that, looking down at us from behind their backs, were three more faces, on a notice-board. They were done in charcoal and even at first glance you could tell something wasn't quite right with them (this was obviously no time to study them more closely, but since I go past something of the kind five times a week, I'm prepared to state that it was probably sloppy shading or something ordinary like proportion).

"We'll have that off, you newts," said the one without glasses.

Jeff tipped his head on one side.

"We don't allow long hair on newts," said the second one and tried to grab him by the hair.

Jeff ducked like a boxer. The final-year boy paused and then went for an alternative, easier target, grabbing *me* by the hair. Jeff scowled, flung one arm forward and seized his wrist.

"Hands off him," he said calmly, but amiably enough.

They eyed each other briefly—and then the one in specs surprised me by letting go.

"Who do you think you are?" the other one exclaimed.

His delayed outrage seemed not to be directed at Jeff—he too appeared to want to avoid direct confrontation. Jeff pushed him gently aside so we could walk on.

"They were trying to bully us," I said, emboldened by Jeff's courage.

"'S right," Jeff smiled. "But they couldn't."

Whenever we ran across that pair in the days to come, they would avert their gaze and pretend to be doing something.

Jeff maintains that our time at high school was one long embarrassment.

"I can't stand those photos. They're nothing to do with the real me."

I find the phrase offensive, though I understand what he means. We were no young Knights of the Round Table—just little fourteen-year-old schoolboys. We couldn't have saved each other's lives or carried out some other such great feat; all we could do was share our lunch packs and save each other a seat on the coach during school trips—but that didn't dilute our friendship. Puberty and the utterly unheroic environment of school may have made it a bit comical, perhaps even awkward in a way, but it couldn't diminish it.

"Memory is life, Jeff," I tell him.

"Yeah, and I can remember I used to wet myself when I was little—but what great meaning does that have for today?"

"So you've decided to forget the embarrassments of childhood and adolescence as quickly as possible... That makes you born somewhere around age thirty."

"Exactly. I refuse to acknowledge those two confused, virginal lads with the same terrible hairstyle, the same disgusting T-shirts with their amateur iron-on ADIDAS labels, who spent their days trying to out-belch each other after drinking gallons of lemonade."

Skippy does a deliberate burp.

"Just because you can't shake off all that banal puberty stuff," I object. "But that's only the props that went with the time. Who cares about T-shirts and belching? Is the massive significance of your first kiss spoilt by the fact that you didn't have it in a prettily manicured French garden, bathed in the light of the silvery moon, but behind the vaulting box in a sweaty gym?"

I'm brought up short—what if I've given myself away by that rather too specific snippet of information? But Jeff takes no notice.

"Did you get to kiss someone in the gym?" Skippy asks with a smirk. "Not very likely—Toady at best, eh?"

I can tell he was about to say *Twiggy*, but stopped himself just in time. Jeff sighs, frowns, and that furrow forms between his eyebrows.

"*Science* has proved," he pontificates, "that every five years all the cells in our bodies get *completely replaced*—which has happened roughly five times since we left school."

He lapses into a pregnant silence.

"So you see what I'm trying to say. Back then it just wasn't us. Not the us of *today*. Almost twenty-five years later."

"You reckon?" Skippy says maliciously, surprisingly taking my part. "So why, twenty-five years later, do you go to Vrchlabí twice a month to see the parents of a five times completely replaced girl you were once at school with?"

Then he points to me.

"And why, a few years back, did this one 'ere marry her spitting image?"

EVA

For several years now Skippy has called round to see her every Wednesday and they watch the football. In the early days they didn't even put the television on; they would chat for a couple of hours and before he left they would look at the edited highlights, so that Jeff and Tom couldn't catch him out—he tells them he goes to watch the match on the big screen at Jágr's Bar on Wenceslas Square with colleagues from the hospital. It was Eva who later told him to go ahead and watch the whole match—she's never been interested in football, but, paradoxically, she finds the excited voices of the commentators quite soothing. At first Skippy pretended to be offended ("Don't we have things to talk about any more?"), but in the end he was glad to adopt her suggestion.

So now he watches television and Eva either sits knitting in the armchair next to him or gets the board out and does some ironing. Sometimes, in the excitement of watching the game, Skippy completely forgets where he is and only when the ref blows the whistle for half-time does he come back with a guilty jolt, then gets up quickly and chats to Eva for quarter of an hour.

"Good God, are you *knitting*? Surely not! Get a grip, you're only forty. What are you going to do when you're sixty?"

On other occasions he enjoys passing the half-time break trying to work out why on earth he comes to Eva's.

"I come to see this fantastic woman—and then watch television. What kind of idiot does that? What kind of asshole?"

Eva knows what's coming. Skippy will skirt past the ironing-board and put his arms round her from behind.

"Why does a bloke come *in secret* to see a woman who's never let him do it with her?"

"And never will," Eva warns.

She tries to make it sound cynical, or at least dry, but each time she blushes slightly.

Skippy sighs theatrically, yet Eva is convinced that he's never really wanted her like that (it's also crossed her mind on occasion whether, for all his talk about women, he might not be gay). He kisses her on the cheek, clumsily strokes her hair and goes back to watch the second half.

It's nicer with the football on, Eva muses. So much better than sitting facing each other in armchairs bought by Jeff, gazing at the blank screen and chatting about dead schoolfriends: Karel, Irena and Ruda.

There'd been a time when Skippy was totally obsessed with their tragic deaths—almost as badly as he was (or pretended to be) obsessed with sex. Time and again he would come back to Irena's suicide: wandering around the flat and endlessly repeating those old familiar things. "What's there to add?" Eva would object. "Yes, we were cruel to her. The whole class. Yes, Skippy, me too, if you must have it for the fiftieth time of telling." Skippy would register the irritation in her tone and fall silent. Despite herself, Eva imagined yet again that moment when Irena jumped. That dreadful thud. She closed her eyes, then opened them again.

"There's no point, Skippy," she says. "You can't be both young and sensible. It doesn't work."

Skippy stops by the mirror in the hall. He takes Eva's hand and draws her to him. They stand there side by side and smile at one another in the mirror. She's fond of him. He looks like a boy grown prematurely old. He stares at his receding hairline with the same stupefaction as if he'd just cut his finger for the first time... By forty he still hasn't ceased to be amazed at the strange planet on which he finds himself. 'What does all this around me mean?' his boyish eyes keep asking.

Sometimes he bursts into silent tears, especially when he's had a drink. He goes bungee-jumping and plays squash. He publishes the humorous *In-house Gynaecological Monthly* (he's brought Eva a few copies before now, but she still hasn't found the courage to open them). He would like to start a family, but he doesn't know how to find a girlfriend. He collects photographs of ice-hockey stars, competition coupons and corks. He commonly uses foul language, which Eva can't abide.

"Today I saw the most beautiful cunt in my life! You couldn't really call it a cunt, it was an orchid!"

"Skippy," she reproves him (Alice will be back from aerobics in half an hour). "Get a grip!"

Shortly after that he falls into a kind of benumbed melancholy. He sits at the kitchen table (made by Jeff), saying nothing and toying with the salt pot. 'Can there be any sadder sight than an ageing classroom prankster?' Eva wonders.

"Shall I put some music on?" she asks.

He shakes his head. From the fridge she gets the first of three beers she's bought for him and Skippy glances up at her with gratitude. Despite her protestations he drinks straight from the can, explaining that it tastes much better than if you pour it out first.

"I'll make some potato fritters, shall I?"

He nods, resigned. He peels the potatoes, she grates them. Sometimes their wet fingers touch. Eva can smell beer, garlic, marjoram—but also senses that agreeable kind of sadness that you get at the end of a good film. 'Or at the end of summer,' she says to herself, that's probably more accurate.

TOADY

"Yeah, I made a mistake, but no one can say I didn't face up to it," Dad tells me.

I have to admit that he really did try. First he went to introduce himself to her parents—he knew the little house on the eastern edge of Prague; there'd been a time when his bus route took him past it. At the very outset he had an unlikely problem with parking: he was terribly nervous and got the completely wrong angle for his Wartburg Estate, and then couldn't manoeuvre in the narrow space between the house, the dustbins and a telegraph pole. He, a bus driver... His future father-in-law, only three years his senior, had to come out to direct him. Behind their curtains, the neighbours were splitting their sides laughing.

"Look, he's trying to back out!" someone shouted.

The bride-to-be's mother was furious—she even refused to shake hands. Thanks to all the bother with parking, Dad's prepared speech had completely evaporated, so he had to improvise.

"Look here, missus, thing's are the way they are."

"Precisely!"

"Life don't always work out the way we want it to. But if we all try hard, chiefly me and yer daughter, obviously, I reckon it'll all be okay."

"You should've tried hard not to put 'er up the duff— that's the fact of the matter!" his mother-in-law-to-be retorted.

Or something along those lines.

His whole visit went on like that, but Dad wasn't to be deterred: he got hold of a pram and a second-hand cot with wooden rails, sold off some of his furniture and converted his living room into a nursery. He bought a double bed, a new toilet bowl and geyser and repainted the entire flat. He started doing overtime to save up for the wedding. The bride-to-be's parents simmered down a bit, but without losing their restraint. The few wedding photos I've found at home still convey an air of tension. Hardly anyone is smiling, and the bride's mother is looking askance.

Dad allegedly came to the maternity hospital every day. It had turned frosty, so his winter anorak must have sent out waves of cold. And in the warm of the hospital ward his cheeks must have regularly turned red. Whenever he could, he would get hold of bananas and mandarins for my mother. I can just see her eating them in silence and, to the limit of her capabilities, thinking; after a while, my father would hold out his hand for her spit out the pips.

"Oh, what a dear little mite! Oh, what a little sweetie!" (or *darling*, *angel*, or other such) mothers whisper in exhaustion as they first set eyes on their baby, their eyes brimming with hot tears.

And now try and guess what *my* mother whispered in the same situation (as revealed to Dad by one of the nurses some years later). You'll never guess.

"Oh dear!"

She left us before I was even three months old.

"Not giving you even a hundred days of her protection!" Boris erupted the first time I told him about it.

Of course, it's often occurred to me that she was protecting herself from herself. 'Nobody can say I didn't give her a chance,' she may have told herself. I'd had almost three months in which to start shaping up. She'd given me three months in which to change at last from a dribbling, whining ugly duckling into a sweet, smiling baby—but I'd let her down: I didn't change. So she left. That was, incidentally, the first time in my life—but by no means the last—when I suffered a severe setback owing to my looks.

Before she left, she took some money from Dad's sideboard and his new Grundig radio cassette recorder, though she did leave him with an open pack of baby formula, a plastic measuring scoop and a feeding bottle on the kitchen worktop. Whenever Dad got drunk and I dared to pass comment, he would always throw these three items back in my face.

"All she left me was a bottle, some baby formula and a scoop!" he would holler, as if that gave him a lifetime licence to get drunk.

In a manner of speaking he was right, of course.

For me, from that Friday afternoon when my mother did a runner to take up with some former boyfriend, she never grew a day older. Today she must be nudging sixty, though on the odd occasion when I think about her, I see her as that confused, not particularly attractive girl more than twenty years younger than me—and that alone helps me forgive her in part.

My father brought my stepmother home when I was five. Up to then, the part of surrogate mother had been played successfully by my grandparents and I was far from desiring any kind of change, but in my child's reasoning I sensed that for some reason Dad wanted me to be nice to this 'auntie' and so I did try (while also being a bit afraid of her). She was a plumpish, permanently grumpy, peroxide blonde. She was the type that spends the winter moaning about the *awful cold* and the summer going on about the *ghastly heat*. When Dad was short of cash, she would complain about the *dreadful cost of living*, and when he did give her some money and she could finally go shopping, she would complain about all those *crazy long queues*. She claimed to feel lonely, but couldn't be doing with visitors. 'With even one person coming, you have to tidy the entire flat, and after they've gone, leaving such a *dreadful mess* behind them, you have to *start all over again*.' Her favourite subject was of course her health problems. That was understandable: she was forty-two and had already had seven different operations.

"Tell me about it!" she would say gleefully as soon as anyone made the slightest reference to their health in her hearing.

She would immediately roll up her slip and introduce the bewildered unfortunate to all her various scars. Time was and I could reel off all her operations, but today I can only recall four: gall bladder, stomach, womb (she couldn't have children) and left eye. She treated me to all the gory details—but then they'd been the greatest events in her life. For two days she'd been *completely out of it.* In the hospital in Kladno the gallstones they removed were *so big that none of the doctors had ever seen the like.* Specialists from all the hospitals in the district came *in person* to look at her. And so on. One day, my father came in from work and caught her lying in her knickers on the kitchen table and giving me a graphic demonstration of what a *lumbar puncture* is.

"Milena, for goodness' sake, put some clothes on and stop frightening the child," was all he said.

When I started school, she took me in hand.

"And now let's 'ave a crack at yer 'omework together!" she would say in all earnest.

She turned the radio down, spread some old newspapers across the table and drew a chair up next to mine. Her voice would be overflowing with good will, though it never lasted the course. Through my first two or three mistakes she still had *the patience of a saint*, but if I made a blot or ran over into the margin for a fourth time, she'd make a despairing gesture, rise and turn the radio back up. I would sit there over my exercise book, feeling guilty and watching as she lit a cigarette and started blowing smoke out of the window.

I was six, but I knew what she was thinking: no child of *hers* would have done that.

"Stop gawpin' and get writin'! S'pose you tell me why you've stopped writin'."

Any child of hers would also be much better-looking.

"On my own?" I tweeted.

"Well I'm not gonna write it for you!"

I also recall moments of a peculiar calm (the calm of resignation, as I'd describe it today) when my stepmother would give all her *if*s, *if only*s and *ought*s a rest and become capable of accepting life as it was—for instance at Christmas or on my birthday. She was a changed woman: she would move about the flat much more slowly than usual, she would stop slamming doors and she would smile more.

"So Daddy and I wish you a very happy birthday, little one."

I'd blow the candles out and she'd take my photo. Then we'd photograph ourselves together, using the delayed action shutter release. We'd laugh. Dad would put an arm round her shoulders. She'd cut the cake. I knew she'd baked it herself, so I would deliberately scoop up the biggest possible mouthful so she could see how much I liked it—except she'd be watching me with rising disgust.

"Don't stuff yerself like that! No one's gonna deprive yer!"

"Leave 'er," Dad would take my part.

She'd look at him reproachfully and sigh. Then she'd get up and start noisily clearing away the dirty plates. And so my birthday would end. The Sunday table cloth would be folded and put back in the sideboard and the table would regain its everyday oilcloth one (with circular black burn-marks round the edge). Her movements would grow faster by the second.

"You're not startin' again, are you?" Dad would say menacingly.

"This ain't no life, it ain't!" she would scream back.

(On the contrary, I'd tell her today, when I'm forty-one, this is exactly what life is.)

It never occurred to her that she was at least partly responsible for her predicament. Had she ever asked herself why the good fortune she laid claim to should actually fall her way? Why should Fortune elbow its way through the stench of cigarettes to fall into the lap of some uneducated frump in curlers with a permanent chip on her shoulder?

I don't think she was bad; she'd just bitten off more than she could chew.

"An' I were that dumb that I meant to make a home for the pair o' you!" she'd often repeat to Dad.

She'd been seduced by the noble idea of doing good—except that doing good had proved more arduous than she'd imagined at the outset. She stuck it out with us for six years before giving up for good.

My birthday without a mum.

Christmas without a mum.

My school report: top marks all round and not a mum in sight.

My first period. And so on.

Do I have to spell it out for you? Is it even *possible* to spell it out? At least try *imagining* it—otherwise there's no point.

TOM

Our form teacher told us about our new classmate in the last week before the summer holidays—the day after Eva, accompanied by her parents, had been into school to be introduced.

"I hope she's pretty, is she?" Karel asked at once and glanced meaningfully at Marie.

The whole class laughed and Marie wagged a finger at him. The teacher half-closed her eyes and took her time before answering. Karel and Jeff were two of her pets; it was clear that she wasn't put out by the question and even back then (let alone today after so many years in teaching), it was obvious to me that this offered a rare opportunity for a spot of harmless coquetry.

"Well, I think she *is*," she said with an impish glint in her eye. "I'd even go so far as to say...," she paused and the class sat up even more, "...*very*."

Very. The power of a single word. If Eva Šálková had been a famous actress or pop singer (which she wasn't, though she looked like one), she couldn't have wished for a better intro before coming on stage. I don't know how the rest of the boys in the class survived the rankling two months of the holidays (back then Jeff and I hadn't started spending the holidays together), but for me it was sixty days of impatient anticipation. Our teacher's dramatic delivery of the information, above all that phrase *very pretty*, had hit me harder than I was ready to admit. With touching naivety I believed that the summer break (consisting of a stint of quasi-voluntary work followed by a holiday with my parents at a borrowed cottage in the Bohemian Forest) was just the tiresome preamble to something unbelievably exciting.

And I wasn't wrong.

The many unwritten rules of the lads' half of our class (we were only fifteen at the time, so it seemed entirely obvious to us that the class consisted of two more or less independent worlds: ours and the girls') included the accepted convention of *bagsying*.

("For God's sake, *bagsying*," Jeff said with disgust, "Don't even mention such daft rituals.")

It is of course an entirely transparent law and up to a point fair; just be the first to apply it at the right point—and whatever tiny privilege is involved is yours. In practice it works like this: if, before the kick-off of an inter-class football match, you shout *Bagsy a penalty!*, you have secured the pre-emptive right to take one. And if, before a school trip, you bagsy your favourite seat in the coach (for example, *window seat* or *the full four* or *at the back*), the others have to respect it. It's all about having foresight and being quick enough off the mark. Everyone knows that the potential advantages in any situation have to be weighed up as quickly as possible—and then bagsied. So lightning speed is the sole guarantee of success; the same idea can come to others at the same instant, so every second counts.

Several seconds were to count for the next twenty years.

On the first day back at school, Eva wore a dark-blue, Wild Cat denim skirt, slightly too big for her (visibly brand-new, given that you could tell at once that the fabric was still stiffish), a thin, white, synthetic-fibre polo-neck sweater and an odd little crocheted waistcoat whose main function—as we discovered with the mute amazement of voyeurs at the first break-time—was to draw a veil over the rather too prominent bulges of her nipples. Any *period* shortcomings in her attire (as I judge them with hindsight of course) merely added to her charms: the stiff denim enhanced the delicate contours of her knees and calves, the clunky waistcoat her spontaneously erect posture and the curves of her back and bottom, and her roll-neck collar amplified the naturally haughty angle at which she held her head, the red of her lips and the clearness of her complexion. My life was at that moment enriched by something that was never to be repeated: a reality that was more beautiful than any dream.

She was introduced to us by the headmaster himself. That's definitely not his custom. I was convinced right then that he'd merely failed to resist the temptation of putting an arm round this extraordinarily beautiful girl's shoulders and walking her down the long corridor all the way from his office to our classroom. The headmaster's presence only deepened the general amazement—but Jeff knew he couldn't hesitate for a moment. He understood that waiting for the right moment could prove fatal. So he *had* to interrupt the headmaster's waffling without delay, right at the start.

"*Bagsy* this one!" he yelped.

Eva blushed and in my eyes became even more beautiful (which surprised me: up to that point I'd treated blushing as basically unappealing, slightly compromising, a bit like sneezing or nose-blowing). Everybody, even the headmaster and our form teacher, burst out laughing and Jeff himself started to grin, but I know he'd been deadly earnest as he staked his claim. The other boys took the same view because the classroom was suddenly shrouded in a stifling air of envy. Damn, how stupid, fancy letting him get in first! I reckon that was the most tragic oversight in my whole life. Like the rest of the boys I made out that I found it funny, but deep inside I was filled with misery and chagrin and hated Jeff with a hate that seers, an animosity that—quite irrespective of the deep, genuine friendship between us— would last for over two decades.

SKIPPY

Incidentally, the fact is that she came into our life without even knockin'. She were brought in by the headmaster hisself—the very same one that every first of September would sing *The Internationale* to us in the school hall. Can you, youth of today, even imagine that? Pictures of Lenin and Marx on the wall and on the dais there's this sixty-year-old, half-bald guy singin' about the last battle that's flared up till the veins on his neck all stand out. Obviously, our form teacher sang along too, but keepin' her beedy eye on me to check I weren't just mouthin' it. This weren't no high school, it were North Korea, tee-hee. Or that time Eva's father drove me to hospital to get my 'ead stitched up: 'Why,' he says, 'do we 'ave such ridiculous nicknames? Skippy and Jeff? Why don't we just call Jeff Jirka? After all, it's a nice name...' 'You don't like Jeff?' I asked. 'Well,' he says, 'I'm not that keen on Americanisms.' 'So why does my Australian nickname get up your nose?' I asked laughin'. Then I deliberately told 'im 'bout the penfriend thing an' that I weren't in the USY. You could tell that got 'im nervous, would you believe! Perhaps he'd got to wonderin' whether by drivin' me to A&E he weren't assisting the class enemy. Tee-hee! My eye were all stuck together wi' blood so I almost felt like a dissident, and I went straight on the attack: 'An' if someone's a lawyer, don't that puzzle you?' I asked. 'What d'you mean?' he asked. 'Well,' says I, 'a lawyer in 1978—that's also a sort of nickname.' He didn't get it an' put 'is foot down. 'Well,' I went on wi' a smile, 'Czechoslovak socialist law, I reckon it makes as much sense as an Ethiopian watch, say. Or Norwegian wine.' 'You can stop that right now, okay?' 'e lashed back, so I knew I'd got at 'im. Wi' my 'ead all bandaged up it were even better. All the way back I didn't say a single a word, savourin' my triumph. The one thing was that I couldn't go an' visit 'em any more. At Eva and Jeff's wedding 'e avoided me like the taxman, but when it started rainin' they chased us all inside them garden tent things, where 'e couldn't avoid me, so 'e came over an' told me I'd been right back then. I'd already 'ad a skinful an' I told 'im I'd never been bothered about politics, and that I thought the wedding were the crownin' event in the sporting calendar. We hugged each other like the best o' friends, tee-hee. Incidentally, the rain went on for five days non-stop—like a practice run for the floods. 'The heavens are weeping,' Tom kept repeating. The newlyweds went off on their honeymoon to France, an' we two were left all alone. Goin' from one favourite pub to the next, we 'opped our way across massive puddles like a right pair o' prats. I can still remember goin' about in soppin' wet socks for that whole week. Tom insisted that if Eva were 'appy, then 'e he was, too, though I could tell 'e weren't at all. Obviously, I couldn't say anything.

TOADY

Every year, right through my school days, my father would insist that on top of the art club, which I'd chosen myself, I should join two others: *cookery* and *sports*. Come September, I'd have this furious argument with him, but not once did he back down.

"You'll join and there's an end of it."

Education by bus-driver, I thought. I hated him.

"But I don't want to!!!" I used to scream.

Father looked aside, because rage, like most other emotions, makes my face even uglier.

"But I want you to," he settled the matter, like in every previous year.

I used to look forward (even at primary school) to art club. I'd always liked drawing and painting and I also like all the smells that go with it: Plasticine, modelling clay, water colours, temperas, wax crayons... I like that moment of silent concentration over a fresh sheet of paper. The only problem with the art club was that we were almost always outside, where, unlike in the classroom, our teacher could smoke (she was about forty, but at the time that obviously seemed very old). Unless it was minus 20 or there was a hailstorm, we would go to the embankment or to one or other of the local parks. We would spread out across the grass, take up any unoccupied benches or settle down on some steps, take out our sketchbooks and she would stroll about among us, cigarette in hand. Having got to me, she would take the pencil from my frozen fingers and correct the odd line, or she'd just stand over me, puffing away and watching in silence as I drew, my teeth chattering, yet another of my big-eyed princesses. Once she even stroked my hair, as if in compassion—at the time I had no way of properly interpreting her gesture of pity.

One spring, we were drawing birds—at least that was the teacher's excuse for dragging us outside in the drizzling rain. However, our feathered friends declined to pose for us, so we ended up using an ancient bird book over whose loose pages we scrapped before the session began. The hesitant Skippy was left with some boring little brown job, so he decided to draw from memory a blue tit sitting on her eggs: first he painstakingly did the nest and in it three little speckled eggs showing random signs of splitting (Skippy took particular care with those tiny cracks)—and then, to everyone's great delight, he covered them with a comically outsize mother bird, but barely crafted at all, because he'd run out of time. The others made fun of him, but I understood: it wasn't important that the eggs got covered over; what mattered was knowing that they *really were there*. That struck me as definitely better than only painting pretty birds and pretending that there were eggs underneath them in their actually empty nests.

Father wanted me to learn to cook for two readily imaginable reasons: for one thing, he hoped that I'd take over in the kitchen and start surprising him with extraordinarily tasty, as it were *feminine*, dishes, which he, as a man, couldn't rise to (he could manage just a handful of *bachelor* dishes that he repeated as regularly as clockwork: pasta bake, smoked pork sausage and spaghetti, frankfurter and lentils, cauliflower fried or scrambled with eggs, fried fillet of cod or pork and mashed potatoes, and bratwurst goulash)—and for another, he believed that my culinary skills might increase my chances of getting married.

I was to let him down on both scores: new dishes arrived to broaden our repetitious weekly menu only very gradually (after a year of fairly lax attendance at cookery club I added only three more items to our repertoire: chicken soup with drizzled egg, fried cheese, and chocolate blancmange)—and because I didn't learn much more even in the three years that followed, I remained firmly on the shelf. He never put it into words, but I know what he was thinking: if I'd knuckled down and learned how to make meatloaf, braised sirloin and liver dumpling soup, someone might have made me his wife.

By contrast, there was no escaping the Wednesday *sports*, which, at least at my school, was a purely formal name for an hour spent playing perfectly ordinary *dodgeball*; my attendance was meant as a *healthy substitute for sowing wild oats* and *to stop me getting ants in my pants.*

"You *are* joking, aren't you, Dad? If I play dodgie, I won't get ants in my pants?"

"You're gonna go and there's an end of it."

"I must be dreaming! You seriously believe that if I spend an hour a week being chased by a ball, that'll stop me having sinful thoughts?"

Do you know what he said to that? You'll never guess.

"A sound mind in a sound body!"

I banged my ugly mug on the table, but my father was adamant. His commands were like papal dogma: just as absurd, just as counter to common sense—and he was just as insistent on them.

Dodgie. Captain. It's possible that for good-looking people with a talent for sport such words in childhood have a magical, sentimental ring, but you can take it from me that we ugly-mugs quake at their very mention even at forty. Dodgeball: you run from one line to the other like a frightened animal, trying to dodge the whizzing ball—and you know that sooner or later one of your own dear team-mates will drive the ball into your stomach or kidneys from close quarters. You let out a funny groan, your face twists with the pain of it, you try to suppress the tears thrusting their way into your eyes, and to the lingering jeering of the other team (and sometimes of your own) you go and stand behind the line. Unlike the two so-called *captains*, you've only got one life, so you're definitely out of the game. I got eliminated too often to count. I was eliminated for years to come. I've been through a lot in life—but such a concentration of human brutality in disguise is not often to be met with. I spent my entire teenage years standing behind the line in humiliation so as not to get the itch. All my teenage years they had to keep hitting me with a ball just to prevent me having a one-off with a bus driver.

The captains would select their teams themselves: the best ones first, obviously, then the moderately competent—and right at the end Skippy, me and Twiglet (in that order). There you have it: my lifetime's role, to be second to last. Not enough to live on, but also not enough for suicide.

Captains were appointed at the start of each lesson by Marta, the PE mistress; most often it was Eva and Jeff because they really were (as anyone could see) the best. Their faces were a picture of silent concentration, their eyes focussed solely on the opposite team. They could catch the ball without even watching it and send it right back into the field of play. Their passes were so quick that I couldn't keep pace with them, and yet they both looked so utterly... unhurried. Eva even wore a gentle, almost shy smile. She never lost a pass by dropping it or having it bounce away (Twiglet and I caught barely one out of two)—as if even the ball knew that its line of flight would inevitably end in the arms of that beautiful blonde. If a pass was coming in too low, Eva didn't bend down for it like me or Twiglet (nor did she let out a groan); instead, lithe as a cat, she would lower her centre of gravity in such a way that her perfect, firm bottom hung barely twenty centimetres above the playing surface (whereas in the same circumstances my own great arse would poke skywards), catch the ball before it could touch the ground, then straighten up at the speed of light-ning and with no obvious effort. Conversely, if a pass was coming too high, she would raise a quizzical eyebrow (You get that? She even had time to raise an eyebrow!), take two or three nimble steps back, rise up on tiptoes, show Jeff, Tom, me and the others her perfectly flat, tanned belly and deftly hook the ball down—my own way with high balls was to jump ponderously upwards as if I was trying to get at an out-of-reach pear. If she had to dodge a shot from Jeff, she would follow its trajectory to the last moment (Twiglet and I would react by squeezing our eyes shut, protecting our faces with our hands, thrusting out our elbows, curling in on ourselves and waiting submissively for the squelchy thud, the burning pain and the deadpan laughter of our class-mates), then she'd jump three feet in the air at the crucial moment, perform a straddle vault or bend like a bow, the ball would obviously pass her by and she—

"And she," as Tom recounted it, "would be back to her fleet-footed running about between the lines, running that had something of the ritual dance to it, she'd cast a mean-ingful glance at Jeff with the result that his combative ex-pression yielded for a fraction of a second and his doggedly clamped lips were brushed by a fleeting smile that flashed all the way to those of us left standing beyond the line to singe our lovesick hearts."

Once, I'd have been seventeen, I broke down and burst into tears behind the line. Irena-Twiglet watched me with disgust, despite the fact that she'd been eliminated before me.

"Stop blubbering, will you, Toady?"

All my helplessness and self-pity suddenly change to rage.

"Sod off, Twiglet, will you, just sod off!"

She was briefly taken aback, but then she came closer. 'How could the good Lord have created something so unsightly?' flashed through my head. Irena looked round cautiously.

"What did you expect?" she hissed. "Why do you keep thinking that life for us two *won't* be hell on earth?"

I caught my breath.

"It *will*," Twiglet said equably. "Life for us is and will be hell. You might as well get used to the idea."

TOM

On a board in the hall by the ticket office it said that the temperature outside was 15°; the water allegedly 19°. I suggested we might pass on the swimming and go to the pictures for a change; Jeff was in favour, but Eva begged us not to give up on it.

"I really *need* a swim," she insisted. "I do!"

Jeff glanced at me.

"Okay then," I said with a sigh.

Eva jumped for joy and kissed me on the cheek.

A cold wind was ripping the murky sky into grey-white shreds. The pool was practically deserted and even the lifeguard had crept indoors; just two swimmers kept passing each other. Jeff and I were squatting with our backs towards the entrance to the ladies' cubicles, one on each side, our teeth chattering, and trying to huddle as tightly as possible into our small wet towels (we never took large bath towels with us; for some bizarre reason we thought them too girly).

"What it says there is bullshit," Jeff said gloomily. "It's 12° at best."

I nodded. In the changing room I suggested we might skip having a shower, seeing what the weather was like, but he insisted that Eva would be able to tell. A woman of about thirty came along, dragging a pre-school kid behind her, blue with cold and wrapped in a bathrobe; she was rushing, but still found time to give us an amused once-over—her eyes settled on Jeff a second longer. I was used to that by then. I was struck by the notion that in that formation we looked like a parody of the stone lions outside some palace. The door to the ladies' changing rooms clicked shut and silence descended anew.

"She'll drive me mad," said Jeff, for a second time.

Me too, I thought to myself.

"She's been ages. What can she be doing in there?"

I preferred not to visualise it. Eventually I heard a rapid patter of bare wet feet. I didn't get up, just raised my eyes: first I saw her arched back and the backwards thrusting bottom with which she was attempting to push the glazed door open—she had her hands full. She too had had a shower; her yellow costume was clinging to her skin. Unlike us, she already had a tan; the few centimetres of skin not quite covered by her costume were visibly paler. She spotted us and her features brightened with a coy smile. The wind played with the pale fuzz about her temple. She came and stood equidistantly between us—as if mere symmetry could furnish justice. As if by not standing nearer to Jeff she might make amends for not being my girlfriend, but his.

"Look, your palace puppies," I cracked before Jeff got up (at the last moment I'd decided to swap lions for dogs, which I thought better somehow). "Bow, wow!"

I glanced at Jeff; he got the message.

"Bow, wow, wow!" he barked in devotion.

Eva rewarded me with a smile so sweet that I got a twinge in my loins.

"For God's sake, come on!" Jeff called.

We all three broke into a run as if on the word 'go', but before we reached the little disinfectant pool we stopped. Eva put one leg forward, stretched her foot out and dipped her toes in the water: as ever, she wrinkled her nose and raised an eyebrow for good measure, rolled her eyes and pouted her lips.

"It's cold!" she squeaked.

Such face-pulling, uncontrollable fits of laughter and, above all, the physical jerks and hopping about in every conceivable manner were the last links to her childhood. I took her huge sports bag from her (*nerve-racking politeness*, as I was to read many years later in Lawrence Durrell's *Alexandria Quartet*) and Jeff took her in his arms. He carried her much further than just the edge of the pool: either he meant to give evidence of his strength or to get as far away as possible from me. He gazed into her eyes, and she returned the gaze—as for me, my attention was drawn to her temporarily deformed breasts and the surprisingly dark hairs peeking out from under her costume. No one was noticing my own peeking hairs. For an age of seconds I ceased to exist. I was standing ankle-deep in some cold chemical solution, shaking with cold and gripping Eva's bag with both hands.

It was the beginning of May, the month of love.

THE AUTHOR

At the age of seventeen the author fell in love with a girl from the year below, whom he used to meet in the corridor as they passed in the breaks between classes: she had long brown hair and a genial smile that could warm his heart for the duration of several lessons. After two weeks he knew exactly where and when he would bump into her and he would prepare methodically for each meeting: this meant rubbing his lips together to redden them, unbuttoning his Grundig anorak, tensing his pectoral muscles and trying to put on a fixed, deep gaze (a friend of his mother's had twice told him how lovely his eyes were). At the same time he would mask his shortcomings, discreetly keeping his small hands hidden (this failing had been pointed out to him by a tactless ice-cream seller in Kutná Hora) as well as the gold, top right crown on his teeth. He knew that his smile mustn't be too broad (it was only years later that he discovered to his horror, in the mirror, that it was somewhat lop-sided). Someone once told him he had an unhealthy pallor, so he started applying a cheap brown suntan lotion before setting off to school.

After two months of twisted smiles set in a greasy face he chanced his first few words with the girl; after that he spoke to her at every break. She would concur with anything he said—about sundry pop stars. Their classmates would turn to look at them, which made him feel good. The girl told him about horses: she was into show-jumping. In the night-time he would dream of initiating her into the mysteries of sex (of course only after he'd learned all about them himself), but during those breaks he did nothing that might have brought that dream any closer to reality.

It was six months later that, one Saturday morning, he donned his mother's branded jeans, looked up the appropriate bus time-table and set off to see the girl. His knowledge about sex might still be next to nothing, but he was mentally reconciled to some version of *sweet bilateral fumblings*. The girl was plainly caught off balance by his arrival: for one thing it was the day of some regional competition, and for another she'd been going out with a married man for over a year. *The wattle hurdles along the track / burst into bloom with toxic meadow saffrons*, the author would write in a poem that evening.

In the years that followed he would switch from verse to prose.

TOADY

As you've probably guessed, dodgeball did not drive the ants from my pants.

On the contrary, my sexuality stirred a few years earlier than my bus-driver father could have imagined: I discovered that little pleasure button at the age of thirteen, a time when at bedtime he (provided he was in a good mood) would still sing *Rock-a-bye baby* and other lullabies to me. This always ended with *counting sheep* together, though that was merely a formal ritual, given that Dad never had the patience to wait until I'd actually fallen asleep. So we only had twelve sheep: as soon as *the twelfth sheep crossed the bridge over the stream* (yes, that's exactly as he said it; today the memory of it brings tears to my eyes), he would kiss me on the forehead, pull the duvet up under my chin, put the light out and go and open a bottle of beer—meanwhile in the dark, eyes wide and with one hand down there, I would wait for the thirteenth sheep. As soon as it came, my big toes would start twisting and I would bleat so loud that I had to stuff the pillow in my mouth.

I remember clearly, down to the last detail, how it happened the first time: that evening, after Dad had left, I rolled onto my back, hitched up my cotton nightie and started thinking about Tom—we'd been in the same class since primary school. Somehow I couldn't quite make out his face, but I had an idea: if I could just conjure up some story where Tom would be involved (after thirty years of practical auto-eroticism I could obviously have put that better: for a fantasy to take hold, the object of longing has to be set in a genuine context). Without much thought I began to imagine, God knows why—and with the best will in the world I couldn't begin to explain where on earth this particular idea came from—that I'm sitting with Tom at the same table in the deserted school dinner hall: there are no other pupils there, nor any of the teachers. Without exchanging words, we're eating rissoles with mashed potatoes and gherkins. I've got my best outfit on, the things I would wear to the theatre and on days when they handed out our school reports: a black-and-red pleated skirt, a white embroidered blouse, a black cardigan and black patent leather court shoes, unfortunately rather scuffed at the toes. Tom's wearing the brand new track suit he's worn that day at PE; he isn't sitting opposite me, but on my right, touching me with his knee. We're being watched by the old dinner lady through the serving hatch.

"Do hurry up and finish, will you!" she says, scowling.

Tom nods his token agreement, but then turns towards me and smirks. His mouth is full of mash.

"Yuck!" I cry.

"Come on then!" the dinner lady persists.

"I'm nearly done!" I call out in earnest (in one sense I'm not actually lying), though I still make no attempt to hurry. The dinner lady gives a gesture of resignation and closes the hatch with a bang. Tom and I exchange glances. The strip lights above us suddenly go out and the whole dinner hall sinks into an exciting gloom. Tom sets aside his knife and fork, turns towards me and slowly pulls my skirt up. Now my white panties come into view. I stop breathing. With his free hand Tom takes a half-eaten rissole from his plate— I should point out that the film of *Nine and a Half Weeks* wasn't made until much later.

"Do you want to see something?" he asks, but without looking straight at me, so he misses my eager nod.

"Yeah!"

He hooks his thumb and forefinger under the lace trim of my panties and draws it towards him. Watching. By this stage I had a sweet, throbbing sensation in my groin area and clasped the pillow to my mouth, but somewhere at the back of my mind the story went on, briefly and sort of as if it was about *someone else*—like I needed to kid myself that the sensual thrill was just a random by-product of the story: Tom pulls hard on the elastic of my panties, the fabric goes taut and from a height he drops the rissole into it.

"Bouncy turd!"

We both laugh. The end.

With the passage of time I discovered that frequent repetition of the fantasy, no matter how subtle, how erotic it was, could take away its power to titillate. By the time the lights in the school dining room went out for the tenth or fifteenth time, the spell had begun to dissipate. I tried mentally *rewriting* some of the details (like by changing what we were wearing or replacing the rissole with a gherkin), which did bring the scene briefly *back into play*—but it remained obvious that this wasn't the way to go. I realised that what was needed was to invent a completely new episode played out against a novel backdrop. Such as: after PE, Tom and I are told by the teacher to fold the volleyball net away and then we (in the deserted, obviously *unlit* gym) get more and more tangled up in it. Or: owing to a number of happy coincidences, the cleaner accidentally locks me and Tom in the classroom for the night. And so on. All these scenes have one thing in common: me and Tom always end up somewhere alone together—and it is always in the half-light, my wonderful lifelong ally. I was fully aware that in the presence of witnesses and under normal lighting Tom would have had nothing to do with me.

In due course, the fact that I let my imagination wander like this night after night, not to mention building up a more imaginative vocabulary, came in very handy: by the time we were in our last year at school, the vast majority of the girls in the class could and did boast of their sexual experiences, so when it was my turn, I didn't have to be awkwardly reticent like Irena-Twiglet. I was prepared. I'd been through so many erotic episodes that I could have started handing them out for free. My infinitely prettier classmates at first looked rather sceptical, but I would casually feed them so many genuine-sounding stories and so many plausible details that the question of my virginity remained at least disputable (unlike Twiglet's; in her case none of us were in any doubt). *How could she have possibly invented all those details?* But I could, girls, you bet I could. There's nothing to it, you just combine the pleasant with the pleasurable... Deep down inside I was quite chuffed that I was such a hard nut to crack: I really must have had a bit of erotic history—even though I didn't *look* as if that were even remotely likely.

TOM

From the start of year three, and on almost right through the autumn, as Jeff and I planned the Christmas break and a trip to the mountains, we talked about taking 'the girls', meaning Eva and Zuzana, with us, *this time for real.*

"Are you mad?" Zuzana said when I put it to her.

I saw her point: like Jeff and Eva, we too had so far got no further than a spot of snogging—and there I was, offering her six nights in a chalet in the Giant Mountains.

"Just *dreaming*, there's a difference. With madmen, men in love and poets it's all non-stop hallucinating."

She was watching me with a degree of interest. I wasn't as good-looking as Jeff, the idol of all the girls in our class, but I did pass for a *clever and sensitive lad*—as Toady once put the commonly held view. I had to admit that this flattering assessment was down to nothing more than three books: Professor Machovec's *banned* biography of President Masaryk, which I'd found by a mere fluke on my parents' bookshelf, a modest collection of Shakespeare's verse, and a slim anthology of Czech love poems entitled *You Passed Through My Dreams* (I knew the last-named practically by heart).

"It's a nice dream," Zuzana said sadly, "but my parents wouldn't let me. And Eva's are even less likely to."

And there it ended; I didn't badger her. Jeff got the same from Eva; he was peeved and cheesed off about it, though I was actually rather relieved.

So we went on our own.

As soon as we got there, we found the stove wasn't drawing properly; and what made things worse, every night and sometimes even first thing in the morning, we had the unmistakable sounds of copulation coming from the next room (though we never once set eyes on the pair in question).

As an opener on New Year's Eve we made short work of a bottle of Hungarian red. We then staggered outside and attempted to build, on the approach road, a snowman with a gigantic penis; fortunately so much grit and wood chippings had been spread that we soon had to abandon this juvenile idea. We weren't much inclined to go back into the cold, smoke-filled room, so we set off through the forest to Žalý Ridge. We didn't encounter a single living soul. It wasn't a particularly frosty night, being around zero, and every now and then some soggy snow would fall silently from the branches. The moon glinted down between the spiky black tops of the spruces. We walked along side by side, occasionally sinking up to our knees in the snow; the going was so tough that we ended up completely sober.

"You passed through my dreams, like a spectre on a stage / as 't were at midnight down an avenue dark you went. / And the mean wreath of blackened foliage / that meant to kiss your brow and aye your hair / is fading now, wilting, and bitter in its scent," I recited slowly, solemnly.

"And?" Jeff asked. "Or is that all?"

I shook my head, to save breath. We stopped.

"I know not e'en your name. I hear your voice / and the rhythm of your steps slumbers in my senses. / And the endless lustre of your joyful eyes / permits me to forget the cold the air dispenses / and the snow that on the trees and in my soul resides."

Jeff nodded gravely.

"We'll ring her parents tomorrow," he said staunchly.

New Year's Day was even warmer and water was streaming down the cracked asphalt road as we descended to the village. I meant to stay outside the phone booth, but Jeff held the door open and gestured me go inside. As he took off his gloves and cap, I glanced at my watch.

"President Husák will just be giving his New Year's message," I said.

There wasn't much room and we were squeezed up against each other.

"I doubt they'll be watching Husák."

"And what if they're having lunch?"

Jeff just grinned, picked up the receiver, inserted the money and dialled—I was a bit dismayed to find he knew the number by heart. He shifted his shoulder and positioned the receiver between our two heads. I could feel his breath.

"Šálková. Yes?"

It was Eva's mother, but the similarity to the younger voice that was so dear to me was so striking that it left a knot in my guts. Jeff said hello and gave his full name.

"Hi, Jeff. Sorry, but Eva's gone off out somewhere."

It sounded quite amiable, almost jolly. At once I had an image of Eva's face, framed by her deliciously familiar white headscarf and bobble-hat, also white.

"Never mind. I just wanted to wish you, and your husband of course, a Happy New Year," Jeff said in the customary manner.

"How nice of you, Jeff. And a Happy New Year to you too!"

"Thank you."

"How are you?" Mrs Šálková asked after a slight pause.

"I'm fine. Tom and I are in the mountains. The Giant Mountains, to be precise."

They chatted briefly about the weather, the snow and the rates charged for using ski lifts. The dirty glass of the phone booth had started to mist over and the wooden floor beneath our nervously shifting feet was now sopping wet.

"And I also wanted to ask if Eva could come with us next year."

This time the pause was a bit longer.

"Hm, I'm not so sure, it's—"

"I thought it better to ask well in advance, so you and your husband have plenty of time to think about it."

Mrs Šálková let out a little chuckle.

"All right, Jeff. We'll come back to this another time."

"Promise?"

Mrs Šálková gave a little squeak.

"Promise me."

The voice at the other end turned serious.

"All right. I promise we'll come back to the mountain question another time."

"Thank you. Good bye."

Jeff hung up and strode out of the booth in triumph. He cast me a glance, broke into a trot and, in ghastly English, sang a loud rendition of *Another Brick in the Wall*. He stopped at the first building we passed, snapped a huge icicle from its snow-laden gutter and bore it erect before him for several minutes as the insignia of his determination.

TOADY

The school corridor during the break before biology: I was sitting on a warm radiator, checking my notebook for form's sake (of course I'd revised everything properly at home) and warming my virginal tush—when an attack was launched out of the blue.

"I reckon Toady's making it all up about that boyfriend," Marie said so that I couldn't miss it.

She was standing by the adjacent window with its view out into the playground, thumbing some dusty geraniums. She was a year older than me and, unlike me, really did have a boyfriend, Karel; they'd been going out together for a year by then. She sniffed her fingers, turned without warning and looked right at me.

"What's his name, eh?"

"Libor."

"And how old did you say he was?"

"Twenty-three."

I managed to quell any panic. Questions of that kind could well have jeopardised the very foundations of my high school existence, but ultimately I was prepared for them.

"So he's a student, is he?"

"No," I replied calmly, "he isn't."

I'd long known what Libor did for a living.

"So what does he do?"

"He's an electrician," I said. "There were no doctors or solicitors left..."

Marie overlooked my attempt at a joke and went on with her interrogation.

"Where does he live?"

"Vršovice," I said sweetly. "On Svatopluk Čech Square. Do you want the house number?"

"No, thanks."

We looked each other up and down. It was Marie who first averted her gaze. She shook her head:

"Sorry, I just don't believe he exists."

Deep inside, I knew she wasn't being malicious—she just didn't like being lied to to her face. She was tall, honest and practical. She and Karel wanted to get married, build a house and have two children. I shrugged.

"I do understand," I replied, slowly, with a smile. "With my face, eh? What boy would want to have anything to do with an ugly mug like me, right?"

I'd already mastered this trick: you say out loud what others are only thinking—and it's completely disarming. Marie fell silent, shamefaced.

"I know he doesn't love me," I went on *serenely*. "I'm not so daft as to think he could even like the way I look."

All the girls closed their books and started staring at us. I relished the strained, awkward silence.

"I know he's only interested in sex. He's always as horny as a sailor after six months at sea."

"And how can you tell?" Marie says finally.

Her aggression had dwindled into distaste. Feminine instinct was still telling her that I was cooking the whole thing up—but she couldn't prove it. While I managed a dry giggle. I was so proud of myself.

"From the size of the wet stain showing on his jeans when we were in the park yesterday."

It sounded triumphant, but somewhere in the bottom-most twists of my mind I realised just how pathetic I was.

"Wait, you mean he came *inside his jeans*?" Zuzana shrieked.

Marie smirked. Beneath the fine down on her cheeks Eva Šálková blushed; her eyebrows shot up and the artery on her slender neck pulsated; at the same time her jaw half-dropped and her perfect teeth glinted wetly. If I'd been a boy, I'd have asked her there and then to marry me.

"Yeah. And we hadn't even got going properly... I'd told him that if he *really* wanted it, he should choose a different bench, because the one we were on had a broken arm rest and there were some bolts poking me horribly in the back—except before we had time to move, he came."

A few more details like this—and I'd have them eating out of my hand.

"And how big was it?" Zuzana asked guilelessly.

This time they all laughed, except Marie.

"*The stain!*" Zuzana cried. "Big as what? As a..."

"As a pie!" Marie snapped, but she knew that she'd lost.

Outside the school I paused for a second and looked back: the homeward-bound pupils from the year below looked so normal, so innocent. The air had a pleasant edge to it and the cracked plaster on the school wall was gilded by the sinking afternoon sun. Could passers-by have any inkling that that warm colouration was hiding from view the little hell behind it?

As I arrived home I was still shaking all over. I might have headed off their disbelief, but only by a whisker. But, above all, for how long? There was something inevitable going on in my life; an oppressive jitteriness was twisting my stomach into knots. I felt like Raskolnikov, but what terrible crime was I actually guilty of? I wanted to be like the others. Is that so hard to understand? I'd probably gone too far—but after that day I had no alternative but to go even further.

"How were things at work?" I asked Dad.

Domestic ritual in the role of safety net.

A grunting noise came from the direction of the television; he'd probably had a bad day, too. I went into the living room and stood behind the ghastly, podgy wing-chair where he always sat (it was *hypertension* that turned me into an interior designer...), then I began to massage his stiff neck. Briefly he resisted, but then gave in.

"Retirement can't come soon enough," he said. "People are pig-ignorant."

I let that pass. His opinions were beyond changing. There was no point arguing.

"Anything happen at school?" he asked automatically, without even looking at me.

Not much, except it nearly came out that I'm still a virgin, though I've been denying it for several months.

"Two A's. In Czech and maths."

Finally he turned to face me. A smile was apt to make him look younger and more handsome. Sometimes I'd ask him why he didn't remarry, or at least bring someone home with him. I tried to convince him that he didn't have to stay solo on my account.

"Are the pair of us missing out on something?" he would reply and it sounded almost menacing.

"No. Not me. If you're not missing something, then everything's just fine."

Dad looked at me with suspicion; the word 'something'

was too ambiguous (dodgeball had done nothing about the ants in my head).

"Absolutely nothing!" There was a categorical finality to his reply.

"All right, then."

"Or do you think I need another biddy in curlers?" he added as an afterthought.

A biddy in curlers. My father's perennial image of a middle-aged woman. His ultimate argument—to which there was nothing to add. Who *could* be missing a biddy in curlers?

"Good," he said in approval of my grades. "And what's for dinner?"

"Chicken soup with drizzled egg," I said, meaning to tease.

After dinner, I locked myself away in my room. I crawled under the bed, where I kept any *nice* cardboard boxes (I was seventeen, but already acting like an old maid!), pulled the biggest one out and laid it out flat. The outer side was printed in colour, but the inside was white. I got some scissors and cut off the two larger sides, then some coloured felt-tip pens from a drawer. It was half past seven and by morning I had to make sure of creating a complete image of my still somewhat ill-defined boyfriend: his build, height and weight, hair, eyes (brown? or perhaps green?), voice and gait. I had to know his collar size and shoe size. I had to be able to describe his parents (suppose his mother was a *biddy in curlers?*) and, if possible, his grandparents as well. Also his habits and hobbies: what sport he was into, what car he drove, what time he got up at the weekend and where he went for his holidays. I had to know what he smelled like, what cigarettes he smoked, and the names of the people he worked with. I had to know whether he snored. I needed to have all his assets and defects clearly defined. And of course there was his way of kissing to be considered, and whether or not we'd be using a condom. Then I had to invent the most common things we argued about and the ways we made up afterwards. And all of this had to be committed to memory.

In short, it was vital that the implausible fictional character called Libor should come to life in my future accounts and show Marie, Tom and all the others... what exactly?

Just how desperate I was?

Just how much I needed a genuine Libor?

JEFF

December 2003: the chairlift was carrying them aloft towards one of the many snow-covered peaks of the Dolomites. The sky was azure-blue. The two pairs of skis (Tom's were seven years old, almost two metres long, while a year before Jeff had treated himself to the latest Atomic carving skis) floated above the broad strip of sparkling snow, lined on both sides by stands of pine trees; just here and there among the prevailing dark green there was the flimsy, yellow-brown crown of a larch.

"So, here we are again," said Tom casually, "back in the mountains and still alone..."

Jeff nodded.

"No girls for company, again."

The wind was cold, gusting. Jeff watched the sturdy tree-tops and tried to guess its speed: above a certain windspeed the chairlift would automatically stop—as had happened three times that very morning. 'At this rate we shan't get much skiing done,' he'd thought to himself fretfully.

"I've always been against the purely mechanical division of human life into decades, but I have to admit that reaching forty does feel like a kind of turning-point," Tom started again. "Life suddenly becomes something that's circumscribed by time. The endless ocean that lay before me even a few years ago has suddenly turned into a village pond. One has to get used to the idea that with the best will in the world there isn't enough time left to get certain things done."

"Such as?"

"Getting rich. Winning gold at the Olympics. Winning a Nobel Prize. Building a log cabin in Alaska. Helping one's son celebrate his thirtieth birthday."

"You haven't got a son."

"That's my point."

Jeff registered that the trunks of some of the pine trees were surprisingly, almost improbably thick.

"Look at that tree trunk," he pointed one out to Tom. "Quite something, eh?"

Tom opened his eyes reluctantly. The freezing wind accentuated his wrinkles, making him look older.

"A fine specimen indeed."

It sounded sarcastic, but Jeff had decided long before to ignore Tom's tendency to scoff.

"The upper terminal's above two thousand three hundred metres. Right now we must be around two thousand and something. Otherwise they couldn't survive here," he said.

"*Here*," Tom described with his ski glove a sweeping semicircle which—as Jeff realised—was undoubtedly meant to embrace more than the craggy massif ahead, "only the strong can survive…"

Jeff grimaced. His posture was quite different from Tom's: Tom had adopted a relaxed sprawl, while Jeff was sitting bolt upright and gazing impatiently all around. For an instant the wind dropped and it suddenly felt warm. Paradoxically the chairlift came to a halt. Jeff hit the smokey acrylic safety shield with the handle of his pole.

"Italians…," he snorted.

Tom tipped his head back and squinted happily into the sunlight. There was still no wind.

"One might expect to become at least a degree more *at ease*," he mused aloud. "If growing wiser is beyond one. Being put at one's ease as a bonus from the Life travel agency. If you miss your connection at an airport through no fault of your own, any decent airline will at least see that you get fed."

'Dear God,' Jeff thought to himself. 'I can't cope with this.'

"But instead things actually get worse. I can sit down cosily with a book, like they do in those old films, but after half an hour I'll have only read a couple of pages. I keep staring at the wall, listening to the trams clanging by, ambulance sirens and car alarms going off."

Silently the chairlift began to move again.

"I could spend an eternity travelling like this," Tom remarked idly.

"Hmmm. Well I much prefer the trip *down*."

"Up, or down. It's all the same in the end."

Jeff had a disagreeable sense that there were now too many things on which his and Tom's views diverged for them to be quite the friends they once were—but he obviously kept it to himself.

"We should get our edges sharpened," he said. "They've got no grip on the flats."

Tom laughed, which really got up Jeff's nose. What was so damn funny about someone wanting to have the edges of their skis sharpened? He sank into a huff. These *poets*, he thought. As the chair rose up towards a pylon his field of vision took in part of the piste. He watched individual skiers and mentally graded their style. And again he couldn't spot anyone who was better than he himself, which gave him no small satisfaction.

At one turn he glimpsed an instructor with a snaking gaggle of pre-school kids behind him: they were all wearing tiny helmets and luminescent green vests.

"Brávo!" the instructor shouted. "Brávo!"

"So their life's taken off," Tom observed gloomily. "Next year they'll be kitted out with schoolbags, and before they know where they are they'll be stuck for eight hours a day on a rickety chair in an office somewhere..."

Jeff tutted.

"... and spending the rest of the day arguing with their partners over whose parents they've been seeing most often at weekends... They're *also* in the club. They don't know it yet, but they're in the same boat as the rest of us."

"Well I think," Jeff couldn't take any more, "that those kids are just learning to ski. That's all there is to it. All that other stuff is just your poetic claptrap."

Surprisingly, Tom seemed to find that funny. Jeff regretted that Skippy couldn't ski and so never came to the mountains with them—even his endless vulgarity might have been better than this. He blew his nose. Then he reminded himself of the recent resolution he'd made not to go pigeonholing his friends.

"Okay," he said. "For now I'd have a couple of goes on the black route; that'll see us nicely through to midday. Then we can take the red down to that tavern we went to yesterday."

He thought his suggestion was perfectly reasonable: if he'd been there on his own, he'd have stayed out at least an hour longer; at one, he would have had a quick prosciutto sandwich in the buffet and then carried on skiing—but still Tom didn't seemed particularly keen.

"Not even Klára drove me that hard. And in her case I at least had some *motivation*."

"Well how about this for motivation: your five-day skipass has set you back four and a half thousand."

Tom looked at him with an air of superiority whose source was a puzzle to Jeff.

"Would you do me a favour, Jeff? Could you avoid using the word *skipass* when I'm within earshot?"

"Sorry. It's a perfectly ordinary word. Everybody uses it, so so will I. You must be the only person in the Dolomites who's bothered by it."

"Possibly," Tom concedes. "And I'd be quite pleased if that were so."

When they got off at the top, Tom insisted on having a *snifter* before the planned three descents.

"Just one nip and we're off," he said.

Jeff first abruptly turned his back on him, but then sighed and gave in. In the tiny bar by the top terminal he quickly ordered and paid for two grappas. They drank them straight off, standing. Jeff headed for the exit, but Tom stopped.

"What now?" Jeff asked menacingly.

Tom looked apologetic.

"I *really must* go to the toilet. I realise I can't keep on trying your patience, and of course I'll understand if you go on ahead in the circumstances."

"I'll wait," said Jeff frostily. "Just be quick!"

"You're really going to wait for me? You don't mind sacrificing a full three minutes of your precious *skipass* on my account?"

"Go!!!"

Jeff was ashamed to realise that his shout sounded pretty hysterical. In Tom's expression something yielded.

"For God's sake, Jeff, we're only here to *ski*..."

TOADY

Something was going to happen that I wasn't expecting: since that scene with Marie, nobody asked about Libor ever again—not even Marie. It was just like when I'd revised conscientiously for, say, history—and then the teacher never even called me to the board. Had they suddenly lost interest? I couldn't understand it. Sometimes I had the blasphemous thought that even being found out would be better than the constant uncertainty. But there was little likelihood of being found out; I was so sure of myself. I could get out of the cleverest trap. I was ready to answer even the most devious question with a smile. It might have gone like this:

Marie (in everyone's hearing): I wonder, did Toady's Libor remember her name-day and get her a present? (Turning to me, aggressively) It was your name-day yesterday, wasn't it?

I smirked to myself indulgently: she was so predictable. She thought she was so clever, but really she was kind of stupid. Did she really think she'd catch me out with that question?

Me: It was, but I'd rather you didn't remind me...

Marie (sweeping the others with a meaningful look): Do you mean he didn't get you anything?

Me: He did and he didn't. Depends how you look at it.

Marie (her eyes fixed on me): I think that calls for an explanation.

Me (with an amused smile): In other words, your suspicions about Libor's existence haven't gone away yet... (with a sigh) So it looks as if I'll have to tell you: somewhere or other he bought me one of those artificial rose things, that aren't really roses but, when you look closer at one, it's a pair of folded red panties. A thong.

Marie (disdainfully): Terrific...

Me: I can spot sarcasm, but you don't have to overdo it because I absolutely agree. You're right. It's not terrific at all, it's embarrassing. He knows full well I don't like red, and can't stand thongs one bit. So it wasn't so much a present for me as one for him—if you see what I mean?

I shake my head and make my exit with a display of contempt.

Except nobody asked me about anything. They weren't interested in any presents I'd got for my name-day, who I'd been to the cinema with or how I'd spent the weekend. On the rare occasion when I mentioned Libor myself (I couldn't deny myself the pleasure given how much I knew about him!), the girls either let it pass or promptly changed the subject. It was unnerving. If they still harboured any doubts, why didn't they come out with them? I'd have dispelled them in sixty seconds flat!

The only one willing to listen to me was Twiglet. Of course that bore all the signs of a quid pro quo: since she was apparently the only one to believe in my Libor (or give a convincing pretence of believing), she expected me to believe in her Mirek.

Every Friday afternoon we'd meet in an out-of-the-way coffee shop at Výtoň, far enough from the city centre for both of us to hope we'd not be seen by any of our classmates. I used to approach our meetings with mixed feelings (poor Irena probably likewise): on the one hand I looked forward to being able to tell someone about Libor at last (how he slept, how he talked, how he laughed and how he tapped his cigarette ash into the palm of his hand...), but equally I was dismayed at the prospect of sharing a table with Twiglet. The most hideous pair in the entire place! Inevitably I felt that the waiter was secretly making fun of us and that the people at the other tables were staring at us—as if we were a pair of blind, deaf-mute or otherwise handicapped girls who were *out on the town* considering ways of facing up to the brutality of life.

In a way that was true.

"You know, Mirek's quite temperamental," said Twiglet, quietly, so that no one else could hear. "It's worst when he's got problems—with his boss or his clients—he never wants to tell me about it."

"Libor's the same."

Just like me, Irena knew that no one was going to swallow any tale of a brilliant, handsome partner, perfect in every regard, so she, too, built his credibility on his alleged shortcomings. Mirek (apart from being temperamental) was short and squat and smoked too much. But otherwise he was great. In the right mood he could be really, really tender. For his part, Libor was irresponsible (sometimes staying out of touch for three days on end, though he knew how worried that made me); then he was also selfish and, last but not least, he really needed to shower a bit more often. Irena smiled benevolently.

Her Mirek was a car mechanic. At some garage way out in Kobylisy or even beyond (note that this was the completely opposite end of the city) he would change non-existent tyres for non-existent drivers. This, then, was what Twiglet and I would talk about every Friday: imaginary people and things. Dreams. Illusions.

"He only ever opens up in bed. I mean *afterwards*...," Twiglet gave a giggle and glanced at me to check that I was taking this preposterous suggestion in good faith.

I nodded.

"Sometimes he can go on talking all night," she added cheerily.

"Yeah, they're like that," I said as *one who knows*. "After sex they're sort of defenceless, but also...," I half-closed my eyes and pretended to be trying to *summon up* Libor's post-coital actions, "yeah, you're right, more relaxed. More open."

Twiglet joyfully agreed. She gladly recognised my superiority, yet sensed that it was a matter not of experience, but of imagination: she'd grasped that I'd been dreaming longer and better than she had. Apart from that she appreciated that I was a notch above her on the plainness scale—I was a decent nine, perhaps even an eight, while she was hopelessly down there at number ten.

"Sex always *uncorks* them good and proper," I said, and we both laughed.

Sometimes Twiglet's tongue unwound and she'd lose control.

"And I always think they look slightly comical—I mean when they're done," she whispered. "Don't you? The way they just lie there with their wotsit all shrivelled?"

'Christ, Twiglet, you don't half talk twaddle!' I think to myself. 'Get a grip, girl, get a grip.'

"He lets you see him naked even after sex?" I asked her, deliberately giving voice to my doubts. "I'm surprised; Libor always covers himself up with the duvet."

Twiglet at once begins to falter. At that rate, she'd never hold out against Marie.

"Oh yes, Mirek as well," she blurted. "I meant before he covers himself up... You know?"

Her eyes craved my agreement—and I generously gave it.

A couple of months later, our Friday sessions came to a sudden stop. One week I couldn't make it for some reason or other, the next week she couldn't. It would seem we were both afraid of proving unable to sustain our tacit agreement called *I know you know I know*. All the lying had begun to be unbearably embarrassing.

We did meet up one more time in July, after the school-leaving exams: Irena had phoned unexpectedly and we went for a short stroll along the embankment. Not a word passed on either Libor or Mirek.

EVA

Gradually she lost her taste for dodgeball. She'd not been averse to all the attention, but at the same time it always made her a bit nervous. In the end she grew bored with it. She was almost always captain, so she was forever being watched—who she passed the ball to most, how she twisted and jumped to avoid being hit by the ball. Her secret disgruntlement was definitely due in part to the fact that from early on Jeff had his sights on her—and not only during dodgeball games. At first he'd tried not to show it, but after only a few weeks he'd made no pretence of being after her. He would enter the classroom in the morning and look at her in a way that made words quite superfluous... It was like when he tried to knock her out of the game with the ball—there was even that same ferocious gleam in his eyes.

With twenty and more years' hindsight Eva understood him. Few would have guessed, but for those entire three years she'd allowed him no more than kissing and the odd grope. She used to like him, yes, but she didn't love him (after the marriage Jeff would occasionally remind her of it and they would laugh at it together). None the less, their classmates, teachers and her parents had thought from the outset that they made an ideal couple. In their final year, everyone took it for granted that they were sleeping together (only Tom and Skippy knew the true state of affairs). One day when Jeff failed to show up at school, the teacher, without ado and in front of everyone, asked Eva what the matter was. When Eva's father went to collect a new car, he took Jeff with him. She would tell herself that she was living the exact opposite of most girls of her age: pretending to her parents that there *was* sex. Yet they didn't know much about him (or even about her). What made them so certain? She had a guilty sense of spoiling things for everyone. But why Jeff exactly? she would ask herself. Should she marry him and have children with him just because he'd *bagsied* her? Or because he was good-looking? Or because the idea was so appealing to others?

She was also embarrassed by the obsession that she unwittingly stirred in Jeff. She'd always taken her own sexuality as something profoundly intimate, except that Jeff, by courting her so publicly, had brought it out into the light for all to see. He'd tried so hard to *get inside her knickers* (as Skippy put it in his proverbially earthy way) that Eva began to feel as if she was parading around in nothing but her panties. She didn't know how best to describe it, but it was like when back in primary school the boys would reflect light spots on her chest; she wanted the ground to open and swallow her up. Without wishing to go over the top about it, Jeff's furious interest in her was a bit like telling tales about her.

Years later, Marie was to tell her what Tom had said at one of the class reunions that she'd missed: "She joined our class—and a ready-made script was waiting for her. The script of a soap opera: a handsome youth falls in love at first sight with a beautiful girl and in the end they get married...

The problem was that she—like the rest of us—was too young and naïve to turn down the lead in that kind of love story."

Eva felt hurt, but she had to admit that there was some truth in it.

For a full four years Jeff and Tom formed an inseparable twosome, joined in time by Skippy. Eva sensed that all three loved her: Jeff obstinately, persistently; Tom secretly, despairingly; Skippy, who seemed up to admitting that he didn't have a hope in hell, most comically of all—he wasn't afraid of making an ass of himself, because he was fully aware that the end result would be the same. He would make goofy, lovelorn faces at her, hurl himself at her feet, embrace her legs and, in the school dining room, kiss the blue plastic cup from which she'd just drunk. He would also pour his heart out to her parents: one evening, she came home from yet another platonic date with Jeff to find Skippy sitting in their living room, sipping mint tea with her mother.

"So, this is her, let me introduce you," he cried, having spotted the surprised Eva in the doorway. "The sun of my days, the dark of my nights. Eva. A terminal illness in three letters."

He let out a heartrending groan and collapsed on the carpet, managing to crack his forehead on the coffee table in the process. Eva's father, who couldn't stand Skippy, had no option but to drive him to A&E to get his nasty gaping, bleeding wound stitched.

When Skippy was given a place to study medicine Eva's parents were even more surprised than she was—and when

Skippy told them a few years later that he was going to specialise in gynaecology, her mother couldn't stop laughing for several long minutes.

Tom was quite different. Eva was impressed by the way he tried to preserve his dignity in the given situation (at the risk of overstatement, it sometimes bordered on the heroic), but on the other hand she never felt entirely relaxed in his company. She felt more at her ease with the garrulous Skippy than with the permanently sullen Tom, who would avoid her gaze and the slightest physical contact, and usually he'd make himself scarce remarkably promptly.

Alice claimed that back then her mother's sexuality had still been *dormant*—and that now it had *gone back to sleep*. Eva didn't know where her daughter got her language from.

"Well I hope yours is still dormant," she would say, wearing the expression of a strict mother.

"Well hoping's all you've got left," Alice smiled mysteriously, so it was plain to Eva that she was bluffing.

"Mum?" her daughter started, drawing the monosyllable out suspiciously slowly. "What bloke do you really fancy? Like which actor, for instance?"

"Goodness me, girl... What a daft question!"

"Well, just tell me. There *must* be one you like!"

She had her innocent eyes fixed on her.

"Or singer."

Eva shook her head with amusement.

"Why won't you say?"

It sounded reproachful, doleful even. Eva drew the hair back from Alice's forehead.

"Dan Bárta," she said gravely after a pause.

Alice scrutinised her mother incredulously, but having established that it wasn't a joke, her face, still half that of a child, lit up with genuine joy. She's glad that I'm still capable of at least *thinking* about sex, crossed Eva's mind.

"That's brilliant! We've got the same taste!"

"And do you know where I liked him best?" said Eva with a smile that couldn't fail to strike Alice as enigmatic. "In the film of Erben's *Garland*."

"Garland?"

"You must know it. He played the water sprite."

TOADY

Whenever I went to visit my dad at the mental hospital, I really looked forward to seeing the trees in the grounds (*look forward* may be putting it a bit strong, but you know what I mean): the century-old limes, firs, spruces, maples and copper beeches. I've always approached life rationally and pragmatically, but in this case I couldn't rid myself of the impression that these fine old trees radiated an immense, mystical, as it were *principled* peace. Do you understand what I'm trying to say? All around were the pavilions full of madmen, psychopaths, dying alcoholics, exhausted nurses and nervous visitors, yet the trees remained utterly serene. They stood erect, the sun glinted through their crowns, the wind rustled in their leaves—and you might almost have thought that this was no place of any kind of tragedy. People die because their time has come. There's no two ways about it. In short, Dad's not entirely happy life had run its course and I, his daughter, was here with him. Everything was as it should be. Except in the meantime I'd reached the building where Dad had been for several months, the trees disappeared, I was surrounded by bare walls, and hardly had I glimpsed the first wheezing old boy through the door of the nearest ward, all illusion disappeared. Can any beech or maple reconcile us to death?

His eyes were closed, but I could tell he wasn't asleep.

"Hi, Dad," I said, touching his arm.

He looked at me, unshaven (*as overgrown as a roadside ditch*, as he always put it), with an oxygen tube up his nose. His pleasure at seeing me appeared unfeigned. I glanced at the drip-feed and sat down carefully on the edge of the bed. The plastic urine bag hanging from the side rail was almost full, so I'd have to empty it for him before I left.

"Shall I raise you?"

He nodded. I was a bit worried because he hadn't spoken yet. I picked up the control thing, gently pressed the button and Dad slowly, to a quiet buzzing sound, shifted into a sitting position—there was something slapstick about it, but I didn't like doing it: I could never hit the right position.

"All right?" I asked.

My father didn't look happy.

"Lower?"

Again all he did was nod. I let him down barely two centimetres, but he winced.

"Too far?"

His eyes said yes. Suddenly it dawned: for a dying man there can be no *good* position. When you're dying, no one, not even your own daughter, can find the *optimum* position.

I eased him back down to the original position and he let out a hiss. Sometimes the pain was genuine, at other times he tended to overplay it; my problem was that I couldn't tell the difference. I was wondering what to tell him about first.

"Guess whose flat I helped fit out yesterday," I said calculatingly and went on to name a director of a well-known bank.

As I'd anticipated, Dad's response was over the top: he grabbed my hand, squeezed it and stroked both my cheeks. 'Goodness, Dad,' I thought. 'I only helped him choose some curtains...' He scrabbled about on the bedside table for the beaker containing his false teeth. The father of someone who fitted out the flats of the top brass of the country's biggest banks couldn't remain toothless.

"You ought to give your teeth a bit of a clean," I recommended.

He gestured his indifference.

"I'm on my last legs so they'll do as they are," he said. "Tell me more about your CEO. I reckon he doesn't go by bus much, eh?"

My director had risen dramatically in a matter of seconds, but I left it at that. I gave Dad a greatly simplified account of my design for that particular interior; obviously, I completely omitted all reference to the *porcelain liquid soap dispenser (design by Bernard Vichet)* or the *versatile Rolf Benz three-seater sofa with no-sag support and fully removable covers in fabric, leather or Alcantara.*

"Don't tax my brain," he'd have said in all likelihood. "A bed will only ever be a bed."

So instead I told him how the *director* and his wife had given me coffee followed at once by two glasses of *seven-star* brandy.

"You did all right, eh?" his false teeth smiled at me in triumph.

I shared his glee, which is perhaps why I stopped keeping myself in check: I put on the guilty expression of a (plain) little girl and licked my lips. Dad looked away briefly—the sight of me like that was probably too much even for him. It was hot in the room, so I was probably glistening all over. Human skin's rubbish, I thought. Barely even third-grade as a material—two flaws per square centimetre. Matt chrome, brushed stainless steel or a good quality plastic, they're horses of a different colour. Or that Alcantara: it's got all the best qualities of leather, indistinguishable from suede, and its Teflon finish prevents staining. If I'd got Alcantara instead of skin, I wouldn't even have to shower. I'd just add some extra teflon. Dad drifted off to sleep.

I left school with distinction (having fulfilled the cliché of the unprepossessing, bespectacled top student to perfection for the full four years at high school). Lord knows why, but Dad had wanted me to study to be a *vet*, but I took a realistic view: every day I saw myself in the mirror, so might it not be pleasanter to look at something pretty at least *in the workplace*, I thought. To that extent, any idea of becoming a dentist or vet automatically fell by the wayside. Was I to spend the rest of my life staring up cows' arses?

I told Dad I was going to be an interior designer.

"And what do you want to design?" he said crossly. "If I want my flat to look nice, I certainly don't need ideas suggested by someone else. A table, a couple of chairs and a carpet and that's it. Designs... A bed will only ever be a bed."

Dad didn't need a designer to *prettify* his bus either: he stuck a bit of burgundy-coloured carpet on the dashboard (both eye and hand could easily tell it was some ghastly man-made fibre stuff with a deep pile), onto that he *screwed* a little plastic nodding dog and some gold plastic crown jewels, and above the windscreen he strung gaudy pennants bearing the coats of arms of all the towns he and his bus had visited. And that was that.

I studied at the College of Arts and Crafts, graduated (with distinction, how else?) and one month later got the very first job I applied for. Dad was knocked sideways—but I wasn't all that surprised. The failed applicants for the job had merely *studied* design, whereas I'd spent sixteen hours a day thinking about beauty, symmetry, balance, proportion and so on ever since childhood—and the other eight hours dreaming about it all. I was unbeatable. Just before the interviews I'd knocked back a couple of shots—and completely steamrollered my prettier, sober competitors.

THE AUTHOR

A late weekday afternoon, spring or early autumn—all he remembers is that when the ambulance came dusk hadn't yet begun to fall. He was at the athletics stadium in Sázava and just completing a training session with the other *juniors* in his squad. They were all looking forward to their cherished post-training kickabout. They couldn't wait. Slowly circling the oval cinder track was one of the squad's veterans, a skinny old boy of about seventy. He was there so often that they barely registered his presence—he'd sort of begun to merge with the environment, just like the tall poplars alongside the fence or the wooden shed they used as a changing room. He never spoke to them—and they never talked about him among themselves; nor, as far as the author can recall, did they ever treat him to any snide, pubertal jibes.

They didn't notice when he suddenly collapsed at the bend before the final straight. It was a while before they even spotted the knot of people: without being able to hear what was being said, they could tell from the way the adults were moving that something was serious. The coach dashed past, but he ignored their questions. The session was plainly over. In the bend lay the tiny body, motionless; the second coach was bent over it. They wanted to go and see, but someone ordered them to stay put. 'And what's happened to him?' 'He's dead,' came the petulant reply. A moment's bewildered silence. Then they started grimly picking over it: he shouldn't have been running seeing how old he was. It was his own fault. Minutes passed. What had been quite fun even a moment before was now just boring. Nothing was happening. The body still lay there. It went on too long for them to stay serious. 'If he hadn't been old, he wouldn't have died.' Some of the boys, including the author, laughed. 'Stupid lot,' someone said. 'What about that kickabout? Come on!' They went with some hesitation to fetch a ball, then set up a couple of hurdles to make a goal. The coach came over and explained in low tones that *now* was not the time to be playing football. He pointed towards the bend in the track. The author, and the others, felt disappointed, almost angry. All because of that old dodderer. 'Why the hell don't they just take him away so we can play, right?'

someone vented their impatience. The coach took their ball from them. An ambulance arrived.

TOADY

Do you want to know what the greatest, *genuine* erotic experience of my early years was? Are you interested in what constituted the highpoint of my *real* sexual life and kept coming back to me years later, in a word that key scene when—in American films—the music grows louder and the strings come to the fore?

I'll tell you: one single kiss.

Our class school-leaving party was to be held at some holiday centre at Slapy—organised by Jeff with the help of Tom and Skippy (though he kept interrupting the other two and creating confusion). Their energy and enthusiasm none the less infected the rest of us—as if we'd only just realised that we'd so far missed out on all the beautiful things that allegedly go with being a teenager and that this was our last chance.

We were to sleep two to a chalet. Tom said that we should form pairs, though that proved less problematic than it sounded. Good will and community spirit hung in the air. Katka, with whom I'd spent the previous two months swapping model answers to potential exam questions, offered me the chance to share a chalet with her; I was very pleased. Skippy tried to take over the proceedings and suggested, in all seriousness, that the pairings should be drawn by lot and *without regard to sex*, but, happily, the others ignored him.

"Stop trying to mess things up, will you?" Tom begged him.

"We'll get something worked out," said Jeff with a meaningful wink to the other boys.

Skippy grinned lecherously.

"I can't imagine why you of all people think you might get lucky!" Zuzana treated him to a scathing smile.

It was plain to see that everyone was up for it, even me and Twiggy (we still weren't on speaking terms, but I could tell).

I couldn't imagine why we two of all people thought we might get lucky.

The wooden chalets were set out in four parallel rows; the season hadn't begun and the thick grass between them hadn't been trampled down yet. The chalets were so tiny as to appear unreal; I thought there was a dwarfish quality to them—or as if they were just scale models of real human dwellings. When Katka and I stood at the door, we could easily reach up and touch the flaking, hot, tin roof. The afternoon sun was releasing the familiar smell of old engine oil from the black-brown planking (every year my dad would take his oil to our neighbour, who had a chalet on the Sázava). Inside it was dingy and musty. The walls and ceiling were lined with yellowed fibreboard and the sill beneath the filthy window was strewn with dead flies; the mattresses were all misshapen and covered in suspicious-looking stains. Lying on each of the two beds was a little, paper-wrapped bar of soap, a towel, seriously off-white and anything but soft, and a ghastly pink bedding set with a floral print.

"God help us!" said Katka, quickly opening the window.

She was wearing denim shorts and a white T-shirt; I saw for the first time in four years that she wasn't wearing a bra (like several of the other girls). I noticed that the wooden floor was alarmingly bouncy. Some voices approached: three of the boys were running up to our window. 'What on earth has possessed them to run in this heat?' crossed my mind. Honza and Karel were stripped to the waist; they knew they could get away with it: their muscles were outlined beneath the skin on their bellies and arms. Skippy was already in his swimming trunks, though he was also wearing a check shirt.

"Hi, girls!" Honza called. "What's your chalet number?"

Skippy started sniggering. He might have taken the exams that betokened his maturity a week before, but he still carried on like a fifteen-year-old, in this case opting to take the question as referring to their bra size! That's how well they knew him. Katka leaned out of the window.

"Why do you need to know?"

"No reason," Honza grinned and, like Karel, stared down her cleavage.

"We might stop by in the night," Skippy announced. "We'll have a lot to get through, but we'll definitely pop by. What do you reckon to that?"

He was crazy, but I was glad he included me in the question.

"I wouldn't open the door to *you* in the night even if I was dying from desire," Katka said.

I laughed along with the others. Katka stepped back from the window, glanced at me and gave a saucy shrug of the shoulders.

"I expect we'll have to barricade ourselves in tonight..."

She'd used the plural, I realised. *We*'ll have to barricade *our*selves in. That was nice of her. We exchanged smiles.

"So, shall we head for the lake?" she asked.

Without ado, she pulled off her T-shirt (she had small, firm breasts) and squeezed past me. I smelt her sweat, and it wasn't unpleasant—unlike all the other smells in the chalet. Katka sat on the bed, drew her large red rucksack towards her, gripped it between her knees and started rifling about in it for her costume. With determination I also started to undress: I'd been on a diet ever since the spring and had done a lot of deliberate sunbathing. My figure was still far from perfect, but anyone should be able to tell that between me and Twiglet there was a difference.

We were still in the water when a new, white Škoda came to a halt on the gravel track between the chalets. Ruda was at the wheel with Vartecký sitting next to him. Ruda gave a brief toot on the horn, then got out with a show of dignity and stretched as if he hadn't driven to Slapy from Prague, but all the way from southern Europe—presumably following the example set by his father. He'd passed his test not quite three months previously. Vartecký was smiling amiably. As if on command, the boys scrambled out of the water and ran towards them. They were all slim and tanned, yet their stampede had an unwittingly comical aspect—and that went for Tom and Jeff as well. I glanced at the other girls: Anička and Jiřina were trying to swim on their backs. Eva, standing dreamily in the shallows, looked like a pretty good copy of Botticelli's Venus. Katka waved to Vartecký, but her broad smile suggested that she and I were probably two minds thinking alike.

"Why do they keep running everywhere?" I hazarded aloud. "I've been wondering the same."

"I've had this idea about what being grown-up is: the ability to walk slowly."

Marie looked at me intently. 'Do I surprise you?' I mentally asked her with some satisfaction. Vartecký stripped—for someone who was over forty he didn't look bad—and he came and joined us in the water.

"From the depths great waves came rolling, ripples in wide rings unfolding," he recited parodically.

"And on the rock by the poplar tree, a small green figure clapped with glee!" we responded like a high-spirited girls' chorus.

Meanwhile Ruda, his car key dangling from his index finger and wearing a frown, was walking round the car and tentatively kicking at the tyres with the point of his shoe.

"Ruda," Jiřina and Anička called out to him, "will you take us for a spin?"

Ruda hesitated perceptibly—probably imagining the wet patches on his upholstery.

"You two? Anywhere you fancy!"

I was prepared to bet he wouldn't be drinking later and that he'd go and re-park the car at least twice—just to practise reversing and to feast his eyes on all the instrument panel lights. I felt like saying as much to Marie, but in the end didn't. Ruda opened the boot and Jeff and Tom started unloading four demijohns wrapped round with spaghetti tubing (they'd have looked a lot nicer if the glass were protected with jute or thick straw) and solemnly set them down in the grass. It struck me as ludicrous: they looked as earnest as if they were handling not cheap wine, but a bomb... Tom raised one of the demijohns in triumph above his head and turned to face us, as if it were a sports trophy testifying to his extraordinary doughtiness—but like anyone who's truly in love I was capable of forgiveness.

"Hurrah!" I exclaimed. "Time to start boozing!"

Until that day I'd hardly ever touched alcohol: I don't like beer, the white wine solemnly poured out for me by my father on a couple of occasions was too sour, sweet liqueurs would only have made me put on weight, and bubbly gave me heartburn. Dad was aware of my inexperience and had shown his concern.

"You realise they'll all be hitting the bottle there," he remarked the evening before I was to leave for Slapy.

"Oh, I don't think so."

He treated me to a look of reproach that carried the message: *I may be only a bus driver, but I'm not stupid.*

"You won't want to find yourself puking in front of them all, will you?"

He grinned and waited. His pragmatic approach was crowned with success.

"No, I won't," I conceded.

"Finally, we're beginning to see sense," Dad said smugly. "So, for one thing: only wine. Right? But before that you have to have had something to eat. Plenty of water and no shots, not even one. Just don't go mixing your drinks. And for another thing: drink slowly."

"And how'm I supposed to do that?"

"Use a small glass. I'm sure you can tell the difference between a 100 ml glass and a 200 ml one. And just take little sips."

I listened attentively, knowing that I was getting advice from a true expert.

"Take a break after each glass and check what effect it's having. In any case, you shouldn't have more than half a litre in total. So it's in your own interest to keep count."

"All right, I get it."

Midnight: for early June the night was unexpectedly warm, with the stars shining bright in a clear sky. Thanks to Dad's instructions I was still sober—unlike many of my classmates, who the wine had so got the better of that they'd staggered off to their chalets. Eda fell asleep on the planking of the terrace right where we were sitting, and Anička and Twiglet, to the amusement of all and sundry, slung the old army canvas that had originally covered the pingpong table over him. Skippy was still more or less upright, but his shirt revealed that he'd already been sick all over himself. Vartecký made to leave.

Ten minutes after he left Eva also rose: oddly erect, wearily pale, winsomely beautiful.

"I'm going for a dip," she said.

Tom tried to catch her eye. Marie stooped over Jiřina and whispered something to her; Jiřina nodded. Cold air drifted up from the water and the flames of the candles that we'd set in pickle jars flickered. Jeff shook his head determinedly.

"No swimming at night, we said. No one who's been drinking can go swimming."

"I haven't been drinking," Eva snapped and ran off into the darkness.

We lapsed into a confused silence: the queen had departed.

"Don't all go shitting yourselves on her account!" Zuzana hissed, but no one offered any response.

An hour later there were only eight of us left on the terrace. The party was over—any reference to *the hard core* would have been pointless.

"It's like when the booze has run out," I said into the silence.

Without a word, Jeff poured me a glass. A little later I was examining my face in the mirror in the toilet block: red eyes, a greasy sheen, little flakes of wine on my teeth and lips—but above all, in unguarded moments, my expression had begun to reveal something bleakly primitive. 'I oughtn't to let Tom see me like this,' I realised. 'But does it really matter?' I laughed, wet my hands and patted my reddened cheeks. The cold water trickled down my neck. Tom's face appeared in the mirror, oddly alien, almost off-putting; having spotted that I could see him, he smiled. His eyelids were puffy.

"Too late," I said. "I saw you. Just before. This is the ladies' loo."

"When before?"

"A few seconds ago. Before you smiled. You were someone else. Someone nasty."

"You're right. Because there's two of me. The nasty me and the nice me."

"So are you going to kill me? Now I've found you out?"

I turned to face him. He showed me a bottle of wine covered in rafia.

"What's that?"

"Chianti. I got giv'n it for pashing the examsh."

That made me laugh.

"You said *pashing*, did you realise?"

His fringe kept flopping across his brow and I turned it back. That was the first time in my life that I'd touched him *for real*. It was the first time we were *really* alone together. All that was missing was darkness. The horrid strip light made me nervous.

"Do you fancy going for a walk?" I asked.

Outside, beneath the stars, I let him have it, all of it: all those chilling truths. He tried to stem the unexpected tide, but I wasn't going to stop.

"You're so inconsiderate, you know," I said, smiling. "Awfully tactless, know what I mean?"

"Hang on, hang on."

"No, you hang on. It's my turn. I'm a bit pissed, which is the only time I can say such things to people. Added to that, you're probably the only one who'll get what I'm saying. So just listen. Are you listening?"

"I'm listening," he said, giving in.

The grass was damp, invisible waves plashed against an invisible shore.

"We both know that what you're doing is what's called exhibiting a *kindly affinity for those less fortunate*," I said.

He blinked at me in surprise, but was too honest to pretend not to understand.

"Good," I praised him. "We both know I'm like the poor car mechanic from a suburban garage who thinks the only car worth having is a Mercedes, while knowing he'll never ever rise to one himself."

I was afraid he might start some banal argument against the comparison, if only to hide his embarrassment. Fortunately he said nothing.

"Another metaphor: when folk from different social backgrounds meet, they tactfully avoid talking about money— do you see what I'm driving at? Do you see now why I said you're all inconsiderate?"

"All?"

He staggered; I had to catch him by the elbow.

"You, and Jeff and all the other good-looking boys."

"Why?"

Of course he knew, he just didn't want to put it into words.

"Because at every encounter you let people see all you've got going for you."

I had to let go of him. And then, in the dark, I bashed my knee against the wooden bench. I sat down on it without comment. Tom collapsed backwards into my lap. I clasped his head to my breast and stroked his hair.

"The dictatorship of charm," I went on. "The fascism of good looks."

Alcohol had given me wings and was teaching me to fly.

"So what's left to me? *Libor,*" I smiled bitterly, "and masturbation."

He tipped his head back and looked at me, but differently now.

"Show me," he said. "Show me how you do it. We can compare techniques."

Our emancipation knew no bounds.

"Are you crazy? I've seen myself in the mirror... At orgasm I look as if I'm having my nails torn out with pliers."

We laughed. He struggled back into a sitting position and unashamedly looked me over. Then he started to fondle my breasts with both hands. I did nothing to stop him.

"Do you accept charity?" he asked.

"Only at Christmas."

He shifted his position and twisted slightly.

"Not even an advance?"

"An advance would be okay."

He kissed me, long and gorgeously.

(Music. Strings.)

He collapsed back into my lap and was soon asleep. I listened to his snoring, at once happy and despairing. I had just driven round two blocks in a Mercedes—to spend the rest of my life going about on foot.

JEFF

It was a warm, sunny July afternoon. They were to meet by the Railway Bridge, and they wouldn't kiss, obviously—it was only a fortnight since Eva had confessed to Jeff that at Slapy she'd lost her virginity.

For that entire fortnight he had studiously avoided her; the prospect of their meeting caused him a strange dizziness, queasiness and palpitations. But now Eva was standing facing him, in sandals and a bright dress with straps, not smiling, quite calm, and with no visible signs of guilt. The wind was blowing from the river and now and again she had to hold the hem of her dress down. Before Jeff could find his tongue, along the embankment came Toady and Twiglet: they'd been heading right in their direction so a meeting was unavoidable. The girls seemed taken aback, but quickly pulled themselves together.

"Well, hi!" Twiglet said with a smile. "You also out for a stroll?"

Jeff said nothing.

"Something like that," Eva replied.

Toady looked them up and down.

"You look like an advert for loans for newlyweds."

Eva shrugged:

"Appearances can be deceptive."

The silence that followed was awkward.

"Did I say the wrong thing?" Toady asked tentatively.

Twiglet pretended to be enjoying the panoramic view of the Castle. Jeff shook his head in annoyance and took a couple of steps.

"Jeff and I have to have words," Eva explained to the girls, raising one eyebrow.

Jeff couldn't believe what he was seeing.

"Oh, sorry," Toady apologised. "We'll be off then."

Lord knows why she'd spoken in a whisper, but it just riled Jeff even more.

"'Bye, girls," he said coldly.

He set off without looking back. He realised he was acting the boor, but he couldn't care less. Eva followed him meekly, but after less than a hundred yards she detached herself and trotted off across a narrow gangway with rope handrails onto a floating steel pontoon. She removed her sandals, tucked up her dress, sat down on the grey steps and sank her legs in the water up to her knees. Jeff was obliged to follow her and that irked him: she'd forced him onto the defensive. Yet she should have been the one on the defensive. The prerogative of deciding where they were going to sit down should have been his.

"I've been waiting for you for three years," he said at last. "For three years I haven't even looked at another girl. For three years I've shown superhuman understanding and patience."

The pontoon was being washed by tiny waves. He'd prepared what he was saying at home. Eva's gaze was focussed on her toes beneath the greeny-brown surface: she looked as if she was counting them. Jeff was disappointed by her response: he'd been expecting his justified, logical reproach to hit home to rather better effect.

"Three years," he repeated, his voice trembling. "For three years you've been saying it was too soon."

He noticed a tremor in his hands.

"I know."

They both stared into the water.

"Don't you think," said Jeff, trying in vain to stay calm, "that after all that it should have been me and not... Vartecký?"

His utter jealousy made it hard for him even to utter the name. A pleasure cruiser was approaching from the direction of the bridge. Eva turned to Jeff and tried to pat him with her hand, but he jerked away. 'I'll never touch you ever again,' he thought.

"Right through the fourth grade you begged me to put it off because you *didn't feel ready*..."

"That's true."

She was going to add something, and Jeff waited. He watched the twigs and bits of rubbish caught between the pontoon and the blocks of stone cladding that lined the embankment. Then they heard the shouting and catcalls coming from the passing boat, but Eva's fair head remained bowed.

"Except I probably didn't really want to keep putting it off. I probably wanted you to do it."

That took Jeff's breath away.

"*You what!!*"

Eva looked into his eyes.

"I honestly didn't want you to wait three years... That's just silly..."

Jeff gaped—he couldn't help himself.

"*Silly??*"

"That's right. I realise it's hard to understand."

"Silly!!"

"Let's forget it."

"Hang on," Jeff begged. "Give me a few seconds."

"I don't want to talk about it any more."

Jeff stared at her as if she were something out of this world.

"Oh no, let's go over this again," he insisted, suddenly resolute. "For three years you kept begging me to wait a while, but *deep down* you didn't really want me to wait? *Subconsciously* or whatever you were dying for me to do it?"

Eva closed her eyes.

"You wanted it despite maintaining something else. Have I got that right?"

Eva bent forward, cupped her hands in the water and doused her bare knees.

"Yes or no?"

"Basically yes."

He studied the back of her neck and her partly visible breasts—and imagined her naked, with Vartecký. In a mad rage he banished the vision.

"We should give you a sound thrashing for something like that," he said gravely. "Or maybe kill you."

"So do it," Eva said in a low tone, without looking at him. "Or stop going on about it."

TOADY

The first class reunion was held at the Baby Bears pub at Perštýn, but I got off the tram early, at Charles Square: for one thing it had always been a favourite stop, infinitely preferable to the never-ending crush outside the May department store, and for another it gave me time to rehearse the basic background stuff about Libor. At St Ignatius' Church I crossed the street and reached the New Town town hall through the park—it was there that my dad had married my mum back in 1962. I took a deliberate detour along Vodička Street into Jungmann Street, where one of those sleazy black-market money-changers that hung around outside Tuzex, the foreign-currency shop, took an automatic step forward—though having taken a closer look at me, he turned his back on me and muttered something to his colleague. I speeded up in spite of myself, but their evil, raucous laughter soon caught up with me anyway.

The reunion had been organised by Marie: she'd phoned those of our classmates who had a phone at home individually, and to those who were still waiting for a landline to be installed she'd sent, well in advance, a telegram. The huge trouble she'd gone to was soon explained: the moment the latecomers finally reached the upstairs lounge she'd booked above a restaurant and the waiter had supplied us all with some cheap, and tepid, vermouth, she proudly announced that she was pregnant and that she and Karel were getting married in a month's time. Karel was smiling.

"Nice one!" Skippy sang out and pulled several funny faces.

A bit later, I learned that he'd got a place to do medicine, my surprise at which was even greater than that occasioned by the news of the wedding—or by the no less foreseeable fact that if Eva and Jeff were to hold hands during the reunion, Tom's eyes would steer well clear of their entwined fingers.

We were almost all there; only Dana and Honza couldn't make it: Dana was in hospital having an unspecified operation (we were nineteen and brimming with health, so this explanation struck us as more like an excuse) and Honza and his parents had recently emigrated to Sweden. Surprisingly, almost two-thirds of us had got places at university: Tom (on appeal) at the Faculty of Education, Eva and Jeff were doing law, and Marie, Karel and Ruda economics. Katka had been turned down by the Film and Television School, but was going to try again the following year. Irena was on an extension course to become a dental lab technician; Zuzana had dropped out of medicine after the first term and was working at a nursery school. And so on. In a very short while there was so much new information to digest that I started getting quite muddled. We placed our orders and the first photos began to circulate: the unknown faces of new friends and flatmates. It goes without saying that during the previous four years we hadn't uttered once some of the words we now trotted out quite casually: *semester, irritating, de facto—de iure, re-sit, exam results.* From the aquarium above the bar we were being watched by some horrid-looking fish. It struck me that many of us weren't fully engaged with the reunion: there was a sense that with brand new lives to live some had only popped along to the Bears for the sake of it. As if a class reunion was something akin to a Christmas show at a primary school— nice enough, but just as insignificant.

The waiter conveyed our orders to the kitchen and returned to his post behind the bar. From somewhere or other he took out a chopping board and a chunk of raw meat, which he then chopped into little pieces and, to my horror, scraped them with the knife into the aquarium.

"Good God!" I gasped, "did you see that?"

"Piranhas," Karel explained apathetically.

We've seen all there is to see, we know all there is to know.

The wine was awful (Klostergeheimnis), but at the time I wasn't bothered: up to that point I'd never tasted a really good wine, so I'd got nothing to go by.

"And I've got engaged!" I announced after the third glass (I was still counting) and made a snide face at Irena.

A bit late I took fright at my audacity. I'd had nothing of the kind planned and then it dawned on me why I'd said it.

Irena blinked in alarm, drew her elbows closer to her body and stared hypnotically at her handbag; I knew she really wanted to grab it with both hands and place it on her lap. Several of our classmates exchanged looks. Marie just let out a sigh.

"No!" Zuzana exclaimed. "Really?"

But nothing could stop me now.

"Oh, yes."

"Well, congratulations," said Zuzana. "And when will you introduce us?"

The probability of her believing in Libor's existence was on a par with her belief in Father Christmas.

"He's picking me up at eleven. So you'll finally have the honour."

This rather unsettled them. They'd never have dreamed that I could make up stories with such equanimity. I wouldn't have believed it myself, except that in a sense I was fighting for my life—and at moments like that people can achieve the impossible, they say.

"So you've got the ring to prove it," Marie averred.

"You mean this piece of gold trash?"

From my middle finger I slid the overdone, tasteless ring with its tiny diamond that my father had given me the previous autumn for my eighteenth birthday and let it be handed round. The girls examined it closely. The piranhas gulped down their meat.

"You mean that stone's a diamond?"

"Libor says it is. I think it's just glass."

"Don't be silly, I reckon it *is* a diamond!" Adélka insisted.

She seemed to know about rings. She'd always been nice to me and had never doubted Libor's existence—it was thanks to her that I'd finally understood what it meant to have *the gift of faith*.

"If it *is* a diamond, then I seem to have been lucky," I said, smiling.

I was feeling smug; even Tom subjected me to a brief scrutiny. I've no idea where I got some of the things I said from. Perhaps I'd dreamed them. Perhaps I rehearsed encounters like this in my sleep.

"How on earth could he afford a diamond?" Zuzana voiced her doubts. "Didn't you say he's an electrician?"

"He could've been rewiring a jeweller's!" Skippy joked.

"No, no, but how could he?"

"Exactly," I said wearily with a bold wink at Irena. "His father paid for it."

"You mean Libor told you so?"

"I mean Libor told me so."

"And what did you tell him?"

I glanced towards Adélka and winked:

"I asked him if it meant I was going to be shagging his father as well from then on."

"Nice one!" Skippy cried automatically.

Libor still hadn't shown, so at eleven-thirty I went to phone him at home from the box outside the department store; his father told me that Libor was in A&E: earlier that evening he'd been playing indoor football and had dislocated his kneecap. He offered to come for me himself, but of course I declined. I went back to the Bears and retailed all this to Marie, Zuzana and the rest.

"I knew it!" said Zuzana with a smirk.

SKIPPY

Actually, it's all about not paying attention. I bet at least half the class loathed dodgie. So why did we keep playing the sodding game? I'd always turn my back and get myself knocked out right at the start. 'Do try, Skippy, you're not *that* useless!' That was Marta, the PE teacher—so young and already such a brute. And what was I supposed to do? Keep running out and back until some ambitious twit got me right in the face from a metre away? Or ask Toady. Either Comrade PE Teacher was blind, or she was a total sadist. Sport's just stupid anyway. It pretends it's well-organised fun, but actually it's got totally out of control. If you know how much Dortmund paid for Rosický, then you must have seen by now that sport is beyond the realm of the human. We sit in front of the telly and pretend we know all about Christmas tree formations and football in the modern age and have no idea at all that money is making fools of the lot of us. Fandom is surrogate emotion. All it does is it takes our mind off what really matters in life. Just like computer games, dieting, floating floors and other such crap. Jeff could tell you a thing or two. He stuck with sport so long that he played his life away. You could be watching some stupid quarter-final and meanwhile your wife's in the bed-room packing her bags—not that I've ever had a wife, or wanted one, that's just an example. God, Skippy, where do you get your ideas from... I'll tell you something: for twenty years I've been following the English, Italian, German and Spanish leagues plus every cup and championship, not to mention the NHL as well, obviously, but I've never really been interested. I'm not a fan; I just pretend to be—to others and to myself. I kid myself that it's fun. I finally understood as much in Jágr's Bar during last year's football championship: after a couple of pints I'd nodded off on the table, and when I opened my eyes again I saw about fifty nicely dressed adult males, including our senior consultant and anaesthetist, screaming in unison at three identical Senegalese on three identical TV screens. So I paid and left and nobody even noticed. Like in those thrillers: the victim's alone in the flat with the criminal and the police ring the doorbell. The criminal makes the woman open the door, but he's standing right next to her with a gun to her head. 'Say a word, bitch, and you're dead.' 'Is everything all right, madame? We heard a disturbance.' 'Perfectly all right, constable,' the woman says with her eyes popping out of her head, but the idiot copper almost always just salutes and leaves. People are all blind and deaf.

TOADY

I was to lose my fiancé in the lock by Střelecký Island.

Even today, twenty years later, whenever Boris and I take the children for a walk to Petřín, I sometimes stop by the stone sidewall of the bridge, lean out and try to catch the image of his face in the muddy water below. Little Anna gets impatient and goes on ahead.

"For Heaven's sake, what *are* you looking for?" Boris shouted to me once.

His voice conveyed the benevolent dominance that he needs to have over me and that I don't hold against him. He was wearing a little hat of grey tweed; that's the very type of hat I've always associated with elderly gentlemen. I'd never have believed that a husband of mine would ever wear anything like it—but it had taken Boris's fancy and I couldn't bring myself to ask him to give it up.

"I've no idea," I said. "That's a dinky little hat," I added with a smile.

Boris glanced meaningfully at Lukáš and tapped his forehead. Lukáš started to laugh, but there was something forced, nervous, about it—like whenever he didn't understand something. I could still sense him eyeing me closely from the side as I led him by the hand across the Újezd road junction. In the park he charged off onto an open grassy area, but every ten metres or so he turned back to check I hadn't done a vanishing act. Boris found this unmanly, cowardly even, but I totally understood the boy.

Towards morning, on the very boundary between sleeping and waking, I sometimes have these strange, horrid dreams. About a week before our second class reunion (this time it was Zuzana who did the phoning round, Marie happening to be in the maternity hospital), I dreamt that our entire class was walking through the Stromovka park, swapping jokes about me and Twiglet. She and I tried to get nearer so as to be able to hear. We couldn't not listen, much as someone with toothache has to keep touching the spot with a kind of masochistic satisfaction... The boys tried to drive us away by throwing the prickly cases of chestnuts at us.

"And do you know why Toady's still a virgin?"

"No. Why?"

They were all grinning in anticipation, even Tom. It hurt, but in an odd kind of way it was also pleasant.

"Because she can outrun her dad."

This time the reunion took place on a river boat with a dance floor—not the best idea (though I admit that I'm in no position to judge these things objectively): there were too many other people, the music was horrendous and there were constant queues both at the bar and the two sets of toilets. Added to that, a third of the time was lost passing through locks, where the disco rhythms and the noise of the engines bounced back off the slimy walls, making it impossible to hear oneself speak. The changing wind kept blowing smoke and the smell of engine oil towards our table. The party began to flag. As its organiser, Zuzana had to face some carping comments and so was getting quite tetchy.

"And how about you, interior decorator?" she shouted to me in the lock by Střelecký Island. "Weren't you supposed to be getting married around now?"

A moment before she'd been dancing and she was still a bit sweaty; the strands of hair at her temples were quite lank. Outwardly her smile was amiable enough, but her eyes were cold. I was caught in a black-and-green stone trap. I discovered that I hadn't got the strength to lie—and there was nowhere to run.

"You and Libor got engaged this time last year, so you should have been married within the twelvemonth, or not?" she repeated.

I lapsed into the silence of defeat. Irena suddenly got up and thrust her way towards the toilets. They happened to be playing *The Girl with the Lemon-yellow Scarf*. How ridiculous, I thought. The smell of oil lifted temporarily, but only to make way for the stench of fish and spilled beer. Zuzana swept the rest of our classmates with her gaze.

"I reckon," she began slowly, with malicious satisfaction rising in her voice, "that the celebrated Libor doesn't quite exist, eh?"

I suddenly realised that I would never see Libor again. Never again see him standing at a fuse board, shaving in the bathroom or smoking a cigarette and flicking the ash into the palm of his hand. My eyes filled with tears.

"I knew it, you liar!" Zuzana screamed in triumph.

One of the other girls clambered over Rudolf, sat down next to me and put her arm around me. I couldn't look up; I assumed it was either Adélka or Katka. She patted me on the back, and that was nice; half-turning to look, I saw that it was Eva. Her beauty had something blatant about it.

"Everything will come," she whispered.

I detected a fruity aroma coming from her mouth and even heard a boiled sweet click against her teeth.

"I knew it all along!" Zuzana cried.

Every cloud has a silver lining: the minute I buried Libor for good, I realised I was free. With *really* no commitments at all. I'd *genuinely* never got engaged, so I didn't have to act as if I was. I had no one to be faithful to.

Accordingly I stopped lounging about at home and started going out now and again with others in my year—to one or other of the pubs near the Arts Faculty (previously I'd turned down any invitations to join them). With perverse satisfaction I took in the eternally beer-stained tables, overflowing ashtrays and the smoke-blackened walls decked with pennants, quirky carvings, naked women, wire Good Soldier Schweiks, signed hockey sticks and framed cartoons cut from a satirical weekly. During the early weeks I felt like a spy abroad. I had a vague fear of being caught. I was afraid someone would get up, point at me and shout: "What the hell's *she* doing here? Can't you see the girl's got *taste*?"

Later on I was surprised to find that around midnight many men began to see something in me—unfortunately not the boys in my class (but then I was in the habit of claiming to be *a bit lesbian*), more those older guys that sat around by the bar. If I wore a low-necked T-shirt or a slit skirt they might start eyeing me up as early as nine.

"Men like me," I boasted to Dad, "but never till after their third pint."

It's at least *something* to go on for the time being, I told myself. If I wanted to be rid of the curse of virginity, the chance was there. At last I began to get the better of my tendency to hysteria. I enjoyed the pleasant certainty of being able to choose—though only around closing time, of course. I would enter those smoke-filled, noisy night-spots with the thrilling awareness that every second one of the drunks in attendance could, after closing time, be my first.

There was no hurry, so I could think things through at my leisure. I was clear that I had to choose from among those who had drunk *just the right amount*: two beers wasn't enough, fifteen far too much. The lads in the department said that alcohol taken to excess could cause erectile dysfunction—they would talk about such things quite blithely in my hearing, which I found at once pleasing and offensive.

"And if by some fluke you do get an erection, you just fall asleep during the action."

"Or start puking all over her, which is worse."

"So you can at least understand how easy it is for some us to become lezzies," I said with a smirk.

I was acquiring the image of a *bit of rough*. As Tom put it: There's nothing more false than reputation.

I gradually learned the grim rules of pub chat: I was usually bored for the first hour or so and the time seemed to drag hopelessly. I would keep my own counsel. I was surrounded by high-flying political scientists, psychologists, philosophers and experts on Chinese medicine... All their claptrap used to get up my nose: shallow half-truths that no one corrected, accumulations of total nonsense, and nobody minded. Where knowledge or logic fell short, raised voices or pathos made up for them. With each successive pint I was progressively less bothered and after four or five I would be awash in uncritical, all-embracing sentimentality (though I was obviously also aware how quickly that could turn into belligerence and aggression). By that stage I would join in the conversation more and more. Whatever I said—like some utter rot about the expansivity of the universe— they'd all nod in agreement. And in return I'd tell even the biggest idiots among them how great they were—and without batting an eyelid. Someone ordered me a fernet. We had the odd hug, or someone or other would keep patting my fat backside, or even give me a sloppy kiss.

I was popular.

Of course, I'd sometimes be asked about my boyfriend. I would invariably produce a sad smile (but ready if necessary to add that I hadn't meant it) and reply that my fiancé had died in a shipping accident. It was original enough for the purpose: no one would have assumed that I'd just invented something like that. In Bohemia the standing of seamen must also be pretty high, because this proved an easy way to ward off randy overtures. A death, even if invented, will bring anyone up short. I was a *seaman's widow*. A woman with a secret. I kept the details to myself.

"Sorry, I don't want to talk about it," I would say on the odd occasion when someone asked. "It's still too raw."

"Sure. I understand."

Isn't human life just one big farce?

Once, while drunk, I shed my self-control and started improvising on the lot of mariners' wives: The eternal waiting. The magic of homecomings... They all fell for it, stem, stern and funnel (sometimes I wonder whether I mightn't actually possess the makings of a writer). Of course, I found the image of a sex-starved seafarer's coming home from some far-flung corner of the Pacific extraordinarily alluring; still at the pub, I already knew that back home I'd quickly stuff my clothes, reeking of smoke, into the washer, have a shower, crawl into bed and follow my fantasy much, much further.

EVA

I'm not into autoeroticism, Jeff used to say. Not that she found it in some way disgusting, no, more likely she was embarrassed at herself.

Once, aged fourteen, she did try it, out of curiosity: she'd had a bath and said good night to her parents, then she

128

quietly locked herself in her room, drew the curtains and switched off the light—and still she felt as if all the familiar objects around her, of whose contours she now had only the vaguest impression, were looking on in surprise and disapproval. She stared into the dark and felt so strange, almost alien, that she soon gave up—and at no time later did she ever feel a need to pick up on the experience. In short, she hadn't started, so she wasn't missing anything—that's all there was to it. During those interminable months when time and again she fobbed him off, Jeff understandably began to think she might be *slightly frigid*. She couldn't hold it against him, nor could she talk him out of it, but ever since that lesson when they'd had Vartecký as a supply teacher she'd known what's what.

Vartecký's entering the classroom was accompanied by a questioning silence—they hadn't been expecting him. Clearly not young, being in his forties; he was tall, well-built if slightly rotund. He'd apparently had a recent haircut (Eva could tell from the pale stripes beneath his sideburns), but his face had at least two days' worth of stubble. Clothes: pale-brown cords and a dark check shirt with the sleeves rolled up. His strong, tanned arms bore a gramophone, two speakers and a handful of records; on the top of this pile lay a battered leather briefcase. With no hint of unease he surveyed the class, almost individually. He radiated an appealing self-assurance and unlike many other teachers he didn't have to fight to assert his authority. Eva's mind was put at ease: she'd always been one to get nervous on behalf of others, so any encounter with someone—how to put it— *self-sustaining*, was a relief.

129

"3C?" Vartecký asked.

"Yeah!" Zuzana flirted back. "That's us!"

He casually nodded, set his whole load down on the desk, opened the briefcase, took from it a huge bunch of keys and fixed them with a quizzical gaze. Little crow's feet gathered by his half-closed eyes. Eva liked the way he wasn't overacting. Skippy pointed at the keys.

"Keys," he said, loud and provocatively, "a popular, widespread aid to the unlocking of doors."

The class loudly vented its amusement and Eva's concern for Vartecký stirred again. Deep down she was afraid in case he couldn't manage the new situation. He didn't fail her. Wearing a serious expression he pointed at Skippy:

"The class jokesmith. Popular, if not fit for purpose where life is concerned."

Eva laughed happily with the others.

Objectively speaking, Vartecký as a supply teacher rather skimped on lessons—he put it to the vote and then with no further commentary, let alone any interpretation, he played in turn the two records that had polled the most: Fibich's melodrama *The Water-Goblin* based on Erben's eponymous poem, and Kipling's *The Jungle Book* (back then, the range available in school record libraries wasn't exactly wide-ranging). At first, a few of the boys, led on by Skippy, tried to fool around, but each time he silenced them with a look—more sorry than menacing. For the rest of the lesson the class was quiet. In defeat, Skippy lay his head on his desk and stayed like that till the bell went.

Listening to *The Water-Goblin* got Eva *quite excited*, no matter how ludicrous that might sound. To this day she can't explain it. She can't tell if it was down to the evocative music and its stirring imagery, or, if not above all, to the presence of Vartecký—but never before had she been affected so strongly. She clamped her knees together and imagined the girl in the poem heading for the lake early on a Friday morning. She saw herself standing there, quaking at the knees, on the little wooden footbridge and waiting, oddly calm, for the peculiar character who would soon drag her down into the watery deep.

She didn't even bother listening to Mowgli. Vartecký fiddled wearily with some papers, rubbed his temples with his fingers, gazed at the grey plaster facings of the houses opposite, then copied some names onto a form. Just once their eyes met: Vartecký seemed to hesitate, but then propped his forehead on his hand and bent back over his paperwork.

The bell went and they all rushed out of the classroom; the Mowgli record was still going round on the gramophone. At the end of any lesson, Eva's actions were always the same, but this time her almost ostentatious show of indifference to the teacher seemed tactless.

"I'll give you hand with this lot," she offered in a business-like manner.

Instinctively she'd adopted a different tone from, say, Zuzana's.

"Great," was all he said.

Eva picked up the speakers and the records; that left Vartecký with the gramophone and his briefcase. Jeff, Tom, Skippy and some others looked on in surprise, but she acted as if it were the most natural thing in the world. They walked down the corridor in silence. Eva was glad that Vartecký made no attempt at the usual kind of jovial conversation.

He made just one little joke when they reached the store-room, but his face remained grave.

"Put it there, man-cub."

For the first time in her life she deliberately brushed one breast against another person; never before had she done anything of the kind. He looked at her and she blushed.

"Thank you."

Eva nodded. She stood there without speaking. Of course she knew that there could be no grounds for her continued presence there, but her expression said that she saw nothing improper in the situation—which only made it the more blatant.

"Load test," said Vartecký.

More a statement than a question.

"For both," Eva added.

She didn't recognise herself. She gulped. Gasped.

"If you don't go, they'll throw me out."

She took a step towards him. With two fingers he drew her chin towards him and gave her a test kiss; she repaid the kiss and then ran off.

"Back then, in the storeroom, if he'd told me to undress, I'd have done it," she told Skippy two decades later. "I'd have done *anything*, see?"

Skippy sank his face gloomily in his hands. He reminded Eva of a character in a strip cartoon.

"So, do you still think I'm frigid?" she asked, laughing.

"But it's so awful!" Skippy exclaimed. "I'd be infinitely happier if you *were*!"

"Sorry to have disappointed you."

"Don't worry about me... But how was Jeff supposed to live with *this*? How could he live with the knowledge that he could never stir even half as much desire in you?"

Surprised, Eva stroked his cheek.

"That's life, Skippy," she said. "I can't help it, can I?"

TOADY

Three years after leaving school, Irena Větvičková committed suicide.

That same evening her mother phoned me about it (the worst phone call in my life) as the first in our class to be told—so unfortunately it fell to me to pass it on to my dear classmates. I downed two shots of fernet and phoned Tom.

"Hi, Tom, it's me. Have you got a minute?"

"Sure."

He sounded a bit cautious, which gave me some satisfaction: I'd make him see at once that my reason for phoning so late was a good one.

"The thing is, Tom, I've got some very bad news: Irena took her own life this morning."

"What? Who's Irena?"

I understood: we'd all forgotten she actually had a Christian name.

"Irena Větvičková of course..."

Suddenly the name she commonly went by wasn't fit for purpose. We were proving each other guilty of years of hypocrisy.

A moment's silence of disbelief.

"That's terrible!"

"Yes."

And sooner or later there was the inevitable question:

"Good God, and how...?"

"She jumped in front of a train on the metro."

From one of Irena's relatives Jiřina learned some of the morbid details, which she passed on to us the following day: the station supervisor had spotted Irena walking up and down the platform to no obvious purpose. And there'd been several trains that she'd *missed*.

Skippy tittered in spite of himself—then apologised hastily.

"You really are such an ass," Marie reproved him. "And you think a bit first before you say something," she added, to Jiřina.

"Christ, let's not quibble over semantics. D'you want me to tell you or not?"

The truth was that we did. We wanted even the tasteless details. They might help us to understand how it was possible that as recently as yesterday morning she'd been our classmate—and by midday she was minced meat.

The funeral (I hate funerals!) taught me things I'd never have expected: for instance that Eva Šálková looked amazing even in a black headscarf (since first thing I'd been forcing myself into a state of maximum cynicism, because I was afraid that otherwise I'd burst into tears in front of Tom and the others and go all puffy). Or that Irena's elder sister was a quite successful pianist; even I hadn't suspected that she had a sister.

"Skippy, did you know Twiglet—I mean Irena—had a sister?" I whispered.

I knew the ghastly suit he was wearing: he used to wear it to dancing classes, and now it was obviously too small for him. It crossed my mind that Skippy was another of those men on whom a suit tends to emphasise a lack of manliness.

"No—did you?"

Marie turned to us and scowled a reprimand, so instead of replying I just shook my head. She even—would you believe it—had parents! I'd watched their quivering shoulders: that it was possible to mourn the death of such a minger with utter sincerity filled me with shameful optimism. I made an optical survey of the absurdly symmetrical composition of the wreaths arranged beneath the coffin—it was as if that crazy event could be given some kind of order. Almost all the flowers and ribbons were white. Chopin's *Farewell Waltz* began to play. What idiot chose *that*? At our dancing classes nobody even noticed Irena. Right there next to me Skippy burst into tears (have you ever seen a penguin cry?), so I dug my thumbnail into the skin between two fingers of my left hand. As I squinted with the pain, it felt like I was in a sixties film: nothing but black and white. I wondered if she'd ever been given flowers by anyone apart from her parents. I'd have sworn she hadn't. I certainly hadn't. Twenty-one years and nary a bunch of flowers—but kill ourselves and we instantly get around fifty. Wasn't there something wrong here? I had this sudden idea: wasn't this actually the last in the long line of insults that Irena had had to take: fifty white *symbols of innocence.*

In other words: we all knew for sure that Twiglet had never had a shag.

After the funeral we moved on to our high school local. At the bar I immediately ordered a double fernet; when I explained to the barman why we were all in black, he made a poor pretence of remembering who Irena was.

"Brown hair, longish. Sort of... meek... a bit taciturn," Katka prompted and we could see the trouble she was having avoiding the word 'ugly'. If people could learn to lie with conviction, I told myself, the world would be a bit more bearable.

"Sort of conspicuously unprepossessing," I said aloud. "Like me."

The class held its breath. I call that *coming out* ! I put on a defiant expression, but it suddenly hit me: Twiglet was dead, so from that day on minger number one was going to be me.

I had to bite my lip because this time I would definitely have burst into tears.

JEFF

Although he'd always been quite fond of Skippy, he'd recently found him getting on his nerves sometimes: for instance, he hardly ever did any of the shopping. He said he could easily get by on the food Jeff and Tom brought in— acting as if that was some kind of brilliant witticism, but unfortunately it was true.

If Skippy did go out to do some shopping, there was always a meaning behind it. If one day he came back with piles of cleaning products, this was indirect evidence that he meant to bring a lady visitor into *The Hole*.

"I see, Mr. Clean," Jeff commented meaningfully at the sight of Skippy's purchases.

"And an air freshener," said Tom.

"And Pronto Antistatic Spray. This is looking serious."

Skippy grinned awkwardly across the bulging plastic bags with the gaudy logo of the Droxi drugstore chain.

"We've met for lunch three or four times," he explained. "So I thought I could invite her here for a change..."

"And she accepted?"

Skippy nodded smugly:

"I must have taken her fancy."

"I reckon," Jeff said to Tom, "that what took her fancy was a gynaecologist who could reel off the entire English, Italian, German and Spanish leagues at the drop of a hat."

"And listens to Country Radio and cuts out the coupons from packets of coconut biscuits."

"She must be an odd girl."

"She's not odd in the slightest! She's called Dana and she's twenty-nine."

"I take it you asked her how old she was."

"Of course. And get this: she's a *cop-per-knob!*" Skippy enthused, syllable by syllable. "A redhead! D'you know what that means?"

"We do," Jeff came back quickly. "You needn't go into details."

"She's gonna have a cunt like a squirrel in the forest park!"

"And just as full of fleas?" said Tom. "A pacient, I presume. Mycosis? Or gonorrhoea?"

"Do you mind!" Skippy protested. "Me, and pull my patients? That's unprofessional! She sells curtains and furnishing fabrics!"

The phrase *furnishing fabrics* caught Jeff unawares and immediately brought back an image of Karel's blood-soaked uniform. Life's all just furnishing, he realised. Tom glanced at the yellowing curtains at the kitchen window.

"Something at least."

Jeff obligingly suggested to Skippy that he and Tom would eat out on Friday and then go on to the cinema. Skippy was initially grateful, but then had a change of heart: he'd actually be happier if they stayed in and *helped out a bit on the conversation front.*

Jeff was afraid Skippy was starting to panic as usual. He noted his abrupt movements and all those macho gestures, but he couldn't rid himself of the feeling that this latest date would yet again lead absolutely nowhere.

"That was a daft idea, Skippy," said Tom. "When your bird sees Jeff, she'll want him instead, we all know that."

"Stop exaggerating," Jeff retorted automatically.

"And the minute I say something, then she'll obviously go for me," Tom added with a smile.

Despite all that Skippy insisted on keeping to his proposal.

"She's crazy about me, so I'm not at all worried by you two," he said, quite sure of himself. "You just be your normal silly selves and that'll put her at her ease. And you keep her glass topped up—I can't, that'd be too obvious. I need you to help me soften her up—tee-hee."

Jeff was even more put off by his tittering than usual. Tom tried to offer Skippy a few snippets of advice:

"Keep what you say to the minimum. After all, you're educated, a doctor even, so you don't have to keep trying to convince the girl that you know what the Mesozoic is or who Ján Jesenius was."

"Jesenius did the first ever autopsy," said Skippy.

Jeff and Tom exchange glances.

"Better keep off autopsies, right?" Jeff said with a laugh.

"Better keep your mouth shut altogether. That's your best chance of success."

"What d'you mean by that?"

"What he means is that you've got a mouth like a sewer and that you often talk utter garbage," Jeff added in Tom's support.

Skippy looked offended.

"And if—God forbid—you do want to say something, say it to *her*. Not *us*. And do look her way now and then."

"That's obvious, isn't it?"

"It is to us, though not to you. Up to now, whenever there's been a girl here, you've spent the whole evening looking at Tom, or me."

"Rubbish!"

"And another thing, Skippy," Tom went on gravely, "do try to steer clear of the subject of cunts this time."

Skippy turned his hands palm-side up.

"We quite understand how hard that is for you," said Jeff. "But you have to see that it makes girls nervous."

Dana was a fairly good-looking, sturdy ginger-top with talc-coated acne on her forehead; she was dressed with taste and considerable care. She wore a wry smile, but Jeff's instinct told him that it was just a defensive reaction: if it transpired that this weird foursome date was just a bad joke, she had a get-out. She remained constantly guarded, even when laughing. Jeff understood. He tried to empathise with her (something he'd tried quite often since his divorce): a loony forty-one-year-old gynaecologist had invited her, a shopgirl, to a party with a high school teacher and a lawyer of the same age. It certainly wasn't easy for her, but he reckoned she was doing pretty well so far. Her demeanour reminded him of Eva when she was driving: she would also try to appear casual as she spoke, but he knew full well that she was actually focussed entirely on not crashing the car.

Dana had scarcely sat down when Tom came out with the suggestion that they should all switch to informal modes of address, which Jeff thought a bit premature, but later had to concede that the conversation had then flowed much more naturally. As usual, Tom was a bit inclined to show off, though he also—as Jeff was pleased to note—tried to create a decent space for Skippy as well.

"When you're twenty, sharing digs can be pretty okay," he said as he opened another bottle of wine. "But at forty-one it's not so much fun. But luckily we've got Skippy here. Without him we'd just perish in our own filth."

"That's true. We call him Mr. Clean," said Jeff.

"Mr. Skippy Clean," Tom added. "It's thanks to him that our bathroom and kitchen literally radiate cleanliness—as you can check for yourself."

"And before you got here we didn't even tidy up."

"You can say that again," Skippy said to Jeff. "I was the only one who did any scouring and scrubbing—slaving away like a bloody Bulgar!"

"You don't have any Bulgarian ancestors, do you, Dana?" Tom enquired.

"No."

"And the bedroom's also completely spick and span," Skippy said with a titter.

Tom smiled apologetically at Dana.

"And who does the shopping?" the girl asked, quickly changing the subject.

"That's Skippy too, of course," Jeff replied without hesitation.

"That's where we call him Mr. Tesco. Mr. Skippy Tesco. And it's not just the shopping—he also *cooks*. Every morning Jeff and I wake up to the smell of coffee and fresh pancakes with either blueberries or a maple syrup glaze. That's Skippy's speciality."

"He's even better at custard," said Jeff.

Dana blinked quizzically.

"And last but not least," Tom went on, "Skippy owns a complete trousseau: eight terry towels, four goose-down pillows and duvets and four sets of damask bed linen. Then four silk dressing gowns, two blue and two pink, a twenty-four-piece set of stainless steel cutlery, a stainless steel waste bin and a BOSCH food processor." "Bosch-gosch," said Jeff. "He's a guy in a million."

Dana was having fun.

"Me and a trousseau!" Skippy objected, but yet again without looking Dana's way. "That's just rubbish."

They clinked glasses again.

"But seriously," Tom said to Dana. "Jeff and I must come clean: of course we're beating the drum for Skippy tonight.

We'd both love him to find at last a girl capable of appreciating him."

Skippy let out an odd whinnying sound. Dana smiled uncertainly.

"A girl who would help boost his confidence, given that we all know that Skippy's a *coy gynaecologist*—no matter if that sounds as absurd as a—say—*quiet gunner*."

"Christ, Jeff, you do talk some guff," said Skippy.

"You stay quiet, right?" Jeff required of him.

"A girl who could rise above his weird hobbies, his vulgarisms, his tittering, in short his general dottiness. As you can see, I'm trying to be as objective as possible about Skippy, even though he's my friend. Do you believe me?"

"No," Dana replied merrily.

"Let me prove it: if for whatever reason you were to ask me about Jeff here, I'd have to tell you in all honesty—even though he's also my friend—that he's a homosexual and zoophilist."

"The zoophilia thing's going a bit too far," Jeff advised the girl.

"It was great," Dana told Skippy as they said good-bye shortly before midnight and she was about to head out for the cab they'd ordered. "Thanks for the invitation."

"You're all really nice," she added shyly. "Honest."

"So do you fancy sharing a shower with us?" Skippy said in Jeff's direction and tittered.

Tom shrugged. Dana seemed to want to say something.

"And your teacher friend, Tom, is he homosexual as well?" she asked finally.

"Not much good, eh?" Skippy said after she'd gone.

"If you mean your behaviour," Jeff responded, "then I absolutely agree."

"She was so damn' nervous and that bothered me," Skippy said in his defence. "I could even smell her vinegary sweat."

"And you're surprised?" Tom exclaimed with some irritation; he was drunk by then. "She'll be thirty next year, she wants to get married and have kids, but so far she's only ever met total idiots—if you'll forgive me for saying so. So her being nervous is no surprise at all. She's running out of time. Who's she going give all the love that she can feel inside her?"

EVA

Ever since childhood she's had an almost *physical* passion for water and swimming, especially in the sea. She also loves the morning freshness of deserted beaches—the cold, flat stones that in a few hours' time will become unbearably hot. She and Jeff go for a swim even before breakfast. At the very start of their first holiday together Jeff has to admit out loud that he can't keep up with her. He clearly can't fathom it.

"I admit I don't have any real technique, but I'd assumed I was fit enough to be a match for any woman, including you," he says, shaking his head with a smile.

Eva knows that he's secretly furious. On a run of any distance or on a bike ride he can beat her hands down. So why not when it comes to swimming?

"You really are good," he says as he wades towards the shore several metres behind her. "How the hell do you do it?"

"She takes after me," Eva's mother explains over breakfast. "I used to race as a kid."

The skin on her neck has begun to grow flabby (Eva catches herself noting such things with a kind of irrational disapprobation). Her father smiles and gives Eva the thumbs-up. He's the same age as her mother, but he looks younger.

She takes her textbooks to the beach with her every day—although it's only August, the start of term is still six weeks away and she's safely taken and passed all the year's exams. This is another puzzle for Jeff. Like his parents, he treats her to a joking shake of the head.

"Drop that, will you, our little swot!" her father tells her.

She sets the book aside. The 'swot' word sits ill with her father. In Jeff's company both parents are often prone to acting in ways she's not used to. She can't help feeling that Jeff's presence has changed them, on the whole for the worse, unfortunately. Perhaps this holiday together isn't the best idea they've had—and it was they who invited him, of course. Eva is lying on a brand new reed mat (her father bought four of them at the market first thing), her eyes are closed and she's listening to the pebbles being shunted about by the tide. The sun's beating down. She suddenly recalls the time at Slapy when Toady had declared that getting a tan was her *tuning* system: *I'm* what you might call *an old banger with metallic paintwork.* She also remembers Irena and, out of the blue, Tom as well.

"Shall I oil you?" Jeff asks.

She shakes her head, but at the same time touches his thigh with two fingers. He bends over her.

"I love you," he whispers. "I love you very much."

She squeezes his hand, glances to see what her parents are doing, and closes her eyes again. The sea is murmuring. Now and again she catches the sound of footsteps grinding on the pebbles, or even the odd whistle or flattering comment uttered in an undertone. Fortunately Jeff's presence keeps such displays to a minimum—his athletic build instils more respect than Eva would have assumed. Unlike the men passing by, she knows just how vulnerable Jeff is in reality.

"Mind your eyes don't pop right out, you ogling scumbag!" her father called out to some guy or other.

She likes to sunbathe, but with none of the antics of the past: when she was seventeen, she'd dash home in the lunch break just to have twenty minutes on the balcony in her bikini... Nowadays, the moment the sun's glare gets too strong, she's happy to retire to the shade of the nearest umbrella pine (the smell of whose hot resin she happens to adore). Most of all she likes those moments when the afternoon sun starts to lose its force and the beach is slowly left to itself; the coloured pinpoints of towels all vanish, mothers gather up scattered toys and the screaming of children falls silent. The surface of the water turns a darker shade—invariably making her think that the sea has somehow become more serious. Even the screeching of the gulls is different from in the morning.

"Come on then!" her mother is insistent, herself impatient to get back to their hotel room, wash the salt from her hair and skin and fix her make-up. By now Jeff has also got dressed.

"You coming?" he asks.

She sends them on ahead. As one of the few remaining on the beach she goes for one last dip. Her father teasingly taps his forehead. She waits till they're all out of sight and heads further out from the shore. Unhurried, she slowly circles a rocky outcrop and bobs on the waves. Returning to the deserted shore, she lies down for a little while longer, though not on the mat now—her father's taken it with them, but on one of those huge boulders worn smooth by the passage of centuries. She presses against it with her back, thighs, palms and feet, as if wishing to exploit every square inch of it. She doesn't bother to dry herself down, knowing that the warm rock and the setting sun can still do the job for her. The early-evening sun seems to her to have more warmth than at mid-day—at any event, she's much more aware of its rays. Half an hour later and she might feel cold, but right now it's just the ticket: she feels neither the cold nor the heat. She's aware of her body, her youth and her strength, but at the same time willingly gives in to that familiar, rather pleasant sense of melancholy whose cause she doesn't fully understand.

JEFF

On 1 October 1988 he began his one-year stint of military service.

Eva went to see him off. They were going from the Gottwald metro station; there were still six minutes to go before their train was due, so they found an empty bench and sat down. Behind them lay the valley. Jeff turned to see: this time he found the sight of all those red roofs, chimneys and TV aerials rather picturesque. Obviously, he thought. It suddenly dawned on him that he'd forgotten to tell Eva how to switch the geyser on and off and how to deal with its commonest malfunctions. He started to explain it all, but had a sense that Eva wasn't giving him her fullest attention. He should have been through this at home, on the thing itself. Too late. He tipped his head to one side and tutted to himself. When all she gets is cold water, she'll have to ask someone. Vartecký?—the first name that crossed his mind. Eva could probably sense his unease, because she took his hand; she even kissed him, quite spontaneously. She hadn't done that in ages. As usual, the rumble of the approaching train put him in mind of Irena. He was prepared to bet that Eva was also thinking of her. They should have taken the No. 11 tram down to the Museum instead. Too late.

In the concourse of the Main Station he detached himself from Eva and headed for one of the ticket windows. He strode erect, his every movement seeming now more resolute, more energetic. He was trying to put a brave face on the things that lay ahead.

"Return?" the greying cashier asked.

"I wish," he said, giving her a forced smile.

He put the ticket safely in his wallet, pushed the hair back from his brow (next day he'd be close-cropped) and stooped to pick up his sports bag. It was quite light; he wasn't taking much with him. Why would he? Eva was waiting a little way off. Those few metres between them only added to the exceptional quality of her appearance. If it had been at all possible, he'd have flung himself at her feet and begged her to come and see him as soon as possible—but that was the very thing he could *not* do.

"*I am ready,*" he told her—just like that, in English. "*Ready for everything.*"

They took the short escalator to the upper level, where they immediately ran into Marie, Karel and little Sebastian. Karel pointed a finger at Jeff.

"Where to, sprog?"

"Slovakia," Jeff replied sourly, adding the name of a town.

Karel's smile broadened at once:

"Me too!"

They high-fived each other at such a pleasant surprise. They might not have been particularly close at school, but it was clear that everything would be different from then on. Eva and Marie were also smiling. Karel glanced at his watch.

"Hang on," he called. "Wait here a sec!"

He ran across to the nearest stall. Sebastian kept his eyes fixed on Eva, though his face still wore a scowl.

"What's the matter?" Eva asked.

"There's supposed to be a model train here somewhere, *one that moves*," Marie explained, rolling her eyes. "But we haven't been able to find it…"

"Look, there's loads of trains over there," Jeff said to Sebastian. "Come and see."

He pointed towards a glass display cabinet with models of all the kinds of express trains.

"They don't move," the child snapped.

Marie gave an apologetic shrug.

"Once Karel's enlisted, because he's married and has a child, he'll probably get posted somewhere nearer," she said.

They'd already put in an application to the military authorities. She reached into the leather handbag hanging from her shoulder and extracted a sheet of A4 with twelve long rows of coloured circles—it took Jeff a moment to realise that each row represented one month.

"We're going to colour one in every day, aren't we, darling?" she went on, turning to Sebastian, who just nodded without showing any great interest. "To help the time pass."

Jeff was touched. Eva didn't have anything similar and certainly wouldn't even bother. He scanned the little circles one more time. 'Christ,' he thought, 'how'm I going to stick it out for so many days?' Karel came back with four shots of Fernet. They drank a toast and quickly exchanged the latest about their other classmates: Tom was joining the army in Mikulov. Zuzana had got married and put on weight. Skippy seemed likely to complete his medical degree. Then it was Jeff's turn to glance at his watch.

"Comrade Private, execute a farewell!" he said to Karel.

For the rest of his life he would never forgive himself for that stupid utterance. Because of it Karel didn't even give Marie a proper kiss. He just made a farce of it.

"Yessir!"

Karel put his arms theatrically round his wife and gave her a noisy make-believe kiss. Jeff stepped aside and Eva hesitantly cuddled up to him.

"Take care," she whispered.

She kissed him, but Jeff couldn't shake off the realisation that they were being watched by countless passers-by. The parting left him with a funny feeling. Meanwhile Karel had picked up Sebastian.

"Come on, a nice kiss for Daddy now," Marie said.

Sebastian gave his father's cheek a lacklustre kiss. His attention was still being distracted by all the hustle and bustle: the man selling savoury pancakes, a squeaky suitcase on wheels, a tiny Vietnamese with two gigantic bags... Suddenly he decided that he would, after all, like to see the model trains in their glass cabinet.

"I don't mind if they don't run," he said in a baby voice so as to sound irresistible.

Jeff wondered how genuine his own desire to have children was.

"Mummy will take you there in a minute, all right?" said Karel. "Or we'll miss our train."

That was the very last sentence he'd ever say to his son: *Or we'll miss our train.* Though obviously Sebastian could have no inkling. He just glowered again and Karel set him back down, now slightly irritated.

"Forward march!" Jeff commanded.

He kissed Marie on the cheek, saluted to Sebastian and glanced at Eva; then he turned about and strode briskly off towards the platforms.

The last sentence Karel heard from his wife was:

And no Slovak girls, right?

Which is why, ever since Karel's death, Jeff was very careful at every leavetaking; thereafter he knew that any sentence we utter may be the last.

"A great success," he would say at the end of class reunions. "Really nice. Zuzana did a brilliant job."

"I've had a really nice time," became his way of winding up a weekend spent with Alice. "Truly. Look after yourself, Kitten. And give me a call!"

"It's been lovely, as always," he would tell Eva's parents as he left Vrchlabí.

"Perhaps I should have married *you*," he sometimes added jokingly to his former mother-in-law, and she would pat his still handsome face with delight.

TOM

I was relieved to see that the battered grey door of the metal locker in the corridor hadn't been forced this time and that the photo of Jana hadn't been defaced (on the previous one she'd had her breasts slashed this way and that with a knife). I examined my walking-out uniform with its gold stripes, the white shirt and the cap with its badge: the odd cheap gain to overlie the daily pain, all that filth, the racket and the stench. I suddenly felt a strange kind of apathy. Slowly, still standing, I hooked off my down-at-heel combat boots (worn by others before me for three years at the very least), removed my stiff, fusty socks, the mud-splattered camo suit and green shirt, tossed the lot in the bottom of the locker, secured it again and headed for the washroom in just my vest and shorts.

"Chemical clean-up, right?" said the podgy duty officer as I passed his gloomy post opposite the entrance.

The only thing I knew about him was that he was a qualified joiner; he looked genial enough, but when he got drunk outside the barracks, he could be quite aggressive. Even quite recently he'd still treated me with the customary old sweat's disdain for a sprog, but since the previous week, when, on the open deck of a truck and against the roar of its engine, I'd recited from memory some ten love poems for his benefit, I'd enjoyed a measure of respect on his part.

"Spot on," I replied. "First-degree."

The door of the nearest quarters opened and a jar of pickled cabbage came flying through into the corridor: it hit the wall with a dull thud and shattered. The duty officer calmly stuck a forefinger in his ear. The cabbage dribbled slowly down the latex-painted wall. A squaddy came running out in his orange, army-issue pyjamas, glanced in alarm at the duty officer, knelt down and started gathering the bits of broken glass onto a dustpan.

"Off out for a shag, eh, sprog?" the duty officer hinted at me with a grin.

The young squaddy looked up. The duty officer tutted his annoyance out loud and pointed at the bits of glass. The lad turned back to continue tidying the mess with rather more alacrity.

"I hope so," I replied. "That's exactly what I've been hoping all these last five weeks."

"A good shag's still the best kind o' poetry, innit?"

I nodded in resignation. The sour small of cabbage pervaded the corridor.

I called Jana from a kiosk at Břeclav station; just as she picked up, I spotted a patrol passing by in their red berets. It struck me as absurd to try saluting with the receiver to my ear, so I merely turned my back on them. I prayed that the sergeant major in command wasn't going to be an idiot.

"Tommy, darling!"

"I can't make it, Janie. They wouldn't grant me a pass."

Silence. Disappointment or relief? I wondered.

"Tommy, I'm going to cry. I really am going to cry."

"It's out of my hands, Janie."

I chatted to her for another five minutes before saying good-bye. I hung up and headed for the ticket office. I was off to meet Jeff.

My first leave—and I was off to a different barracks.

THE AUTHOR

The news of the death of his classmate Jindřich (he'd died tragically in a road traffic accident while on military service) reached the author just as he was shifting a delivery of coal by the garage in front of his parents' house. He saw the post-woman approaching the gate and so he disappeared into the cellar for a moment; he didn't want her to see him with his hair unwashed and wearing a filthy green puffer jacket that reeked of sulphur. He listened out for the sound of the letter-box lid—and, sure enough, it came, leaving him inevitably with that joyful expectation of some *important news* (in his heart of hearts he knew he'd absolutely no grounds for optimism in that regard, given that to date he'd never done a single thing that might lead to any such news). In the box there was a white envelope. He spotted at once the black edging showing through—he was no graphic designer, but he did have a sense of proportion and had always thought the thickness of the edging almost vulgar. He opened the envelope... but how? With suspicion? Maybe. *JINDŘICH NEJEDLÝ. All you ever wished for expires now.*

In the first few seconds he felt a defiant, disgusted kind of jollity, by which he sought to negate the news. No, it's nonsense. He read the death notice a second time and grasped that it was for real. Yes, he was dead. So what now? He tried to summon up some emotion, but at that moment none was forthcoming. For his own benefit he rather overplayed the grief thing, clearing his nose of coal dust in the process. What should he do? Leave the coal for now? Should he tell his father he hadn't finished shifting the coal into the cellar because his mate from school had just died? He folded the notice back into its envelope, stuffed it into a pocket of his puffer and gripped the shovel. One down, how many to go? he realised.

EVA

In mid-November 1988, Marie popped in on her way to aerobics: she was going to Slovakia the following Saturday to visit Karel, and would Eva like to go with her?

Eva tried to think of an excuse: though she'd promised Jeff that she'd definitely come in November (she'd had to defer one previously arranged visit, so she'd have to go to Slovakia one weekend soon anyway), but she was also put off by the idea of spending that entire long journey with Marie of all people. It wasn't that she didn't like her, more that they didn't have a lot in common and she was afraid they mightn't have much to talk about. Things might not have been helped by Marie's shell suit and the huge sports bag slung over her shoulder: although Eva was innately sympathetic to movement, the world of sport was alien to her.

"Do come," Marie urged. "It'll be great travelling together."

"Aren't you taking Sebastian with you?"

In Eva's eyes, Sebastian was an additional problem. She'd been through it endless times before: in her presence,

children of his age invariably maintained a sullen silence—
then after huge effort on her part she'd win them round,
only to have them fall head over heels in love with her.
They'd cling to her, sit on her lap, tickle her non-stop and
insist on combing her hair.

"No, his gran's going to baby-sit. We want to get a hotel
for the night, see?"

Eva nodded shyly.

"This'll be our first chance to have sex since he joined up,"
Marie added, forthright as ever. "Have you managed it yet?"

"No," said Eva, blushing.

"There you are then. Come with me."

In the end, the journey was more enjoyable than she'd
anticipated. Of course they attracted attention—but, there
being two of them, things that at other times Eva found
acutely embarrassing, all the catcalls, the lingering looks and
other tokens of admiration, she now found quite amusing.
She happily tried visualising Marie and herself through
male eyes: one an attractive, tall brunette, the other, only
slightly shorter, a pretty blonde... They paid the supplement
for reserved seats, but then spent almost the entire time in
the dining car, where the staff only spoke Hungarian. They
had lunch and three beers each, which was Eva's personal
record. They found almost everything funny: the elderly
waiter, the little pink, tassled lamps over the tables, the
names of the stations and even some of the people waiting
on platforms. And they kept giggling like two little girls.

Marie having popped to the toilet, Eva gazed out at the
passing countryside. Life can be brilliant sometimes, she
mused and determined to do her utmost to make her visit

to Jeff a success. Mentally she tried guessing what the hotel would be like, the one where they'd booked rooms for the night. Never before had she had a one-night stay in a hotel. She wondered if the receptionist would be a man or a woman. She was slightly worried that the bed linen mightn't be genuinely clean and the plughole in the shower might be clogged with hair, and things like that—but equally the whole prospect left her quite excited. Marie was on the way back: with a grunt she tugged open the communicating door between the carriages, so the dining car was briefly invaded by the din of the wheels. She glanced at Eva, pursed her lips and only then did she, conspicuously slowly, do up the zip of her jeans, the Hungarian waiter brazenly eyeing her every move. Eva hid her face in her hands and watched Marie through a chink between her fingers.

"Think about it," she said after a moment, "doesn't it feel a bit as if we're going there like lambs to the slaughter?"

"Don't be silly!" Marie squeaked.

They leaned across to each other, touched foreheads, and their shoulders shook with laughter. A thought struck Eva: If Marie were to kiss me right now, I wouldn't resist.

They reached their destination thirty minutes late, which they didn't think was too bad.

"If we've done without sex for seven weeks, another half-hour isn't going to kill us," said Marie, perhaps a little too loud.

The barracks and the hotel in question were out on the edge of town; in her handbag Eva did have the number of the bus that might have taken them there, but on a whim they took the only taxi waiting outside the station instead. The elderly, obese cabby had a fresh plaster on his right temple. Marie had a stab at speaking Slovak, though Eva wasn't sure whether the fat guy might not see it as mickey-taking—but his response was unequivocally amicable.

"Hev you got some Slovak sonks?" Marie more or less managed, pointing to the car radio. "Corregtion: songs? Like by Elán?"

Eva scowled at her, but the cab driver was glad to oblige. By the time they were approaching the barracks, all three of them were belting out *Dancing Girls from Lúčnica*.

They passed through a gateway in a wall topped by no less than three lines of barbed wire. The wall had been freshly whitewashed: it literally gleamed and in the dry grass at its foot gobbets of lime were still visible. Also new-looking, if amateurish, was the paintwork on the red-and-white striped barrier; beyond that, a vast area of asphalt opened out, embellished with lots of arrows, numbers and unintelligible abbreviations; set in the middle was a comical little island of green surrounded by a red-and-white kerb. A cross between a state border and an airfield, Eva thought. On the roof of the nearest building was a banner bearing the familiar slogan about being prepared to construct and defend the socialist homeland—in Slovak it sounded unusual, almost a parody of itself. From the low, cube-shaped building to the left came a young soldier, presumably the duty officer, who headed uncertainly towards them; he was holding a well-worn school exercise book and a pencil. His uniform was tarted up with some thick red braids tipped with gold cartridge cases—Eva appreciated that the outfit wasn't an expression of the man's own taste, but she still couldn't check a smile of compassion. That disconcerted him even more. Those braids are atrocious, Eva thought to herself. The aesthetics of primitive tribes. Marie gave the man Karel and Jeff's surnames and ranks and he jotted them down in his notebook; then he showed them where to wait.

"He ought to be a waiter," Eva whispered to Marie. "More than one order and he'd have to write it all down."

They laughed, but not breezily as in the train or the taxi. The reception area formed a square, with wooden benches and tables spaced out along the sides. Without their touching a single light switch, a fluorescent tube on the ceiling sprang into life with that familiar buzzing sound. Eva thought it odd, given there was no one else present. It was Saturday afternoon—didn't other soldiers also have visitors coming? Cautiously, they looked about them: to the left there was a small window into the guard-room; it reminded them of the serving hatch in a school dinner room, but there seemed to be no way of opening it. The soldier with the braids, plus one other, taller, were watching them quite openly: behind glass, the young lad on duty looked more self-assured than he had outside. He whispered something to his colleague (Eva noted that he had a broken front tooth) and finally picked up the phone. A shivering sensation made Marie rub her forearms, and she looked about for any source of heat: high up on the end wall she spotted an electric heater, the power cable from which led down into the guardroom.

"Shouldn't we ask them to switch it on?" she whispered.

She'd barely finished the sentence when a low purring sound started and the previously black element slowly started to glow. Marie turned to the window and gave the soldiers the thumbs-up.

By the time an hour had elapsed the little room was far too warm for comfort: Eva and Marie had removed their jumpers long before, and were now in just their cotton T-shirts (they realised, of course, that that was exactly what the soldiers had meant to achieve), and yet they were still starting to perspire. Eva spotted the flashing blue reflection of the light of an ambulance approaching the main gate; its siren was switched off. The taller soldier went and raised the barrier and the ambulance drove in. As yet, no one had bothered to explain why they were having such a long wait. Three times in all they asked the guard whether he really had sent for Karel and Jeff, and each time he just nodded.

"So why aren't they here yet?"

"I don't know."

The girls had no idea what they were supposed to do. The two soldiers were now avoiding their gaze. When they demanded to speak to the men's superior officer, they were told that that was not possible. Eva felt powerless. The heat was unbearable. In annoyance, she got up, tapped on the window and pointed to the heater; she made a gesture of taking the plug out of the socket. They eyed up her frontage, but then did unplug the heater.

"Well that's something," said Marie.

An older soldier with greying hair looked into the room and fixed them with a vacant expression.

"Hello," said Eva, jumping up from her chair. "We've come to visit, and for some reason we've been kept waiting an awful long time."

The soldier left without responding. Marie flung her arms wide:

"This is driving me mad!"

Outside it was starting to get dark, the lights in the yard were coming on and a yellowy-orange light descended onto the asphalt. 'This trip isn't going right,' Eva mused.

After another twenty minutes, which they spent impatiently crossing the room this way and that and staring out of the window, a white Lada 1200 drove up from the direction of the main buildings; two soldiers alighted from it and Eva assumed, from their epaulettes and the stripes on their trousers, that they must be officers. The guard and the other soldier ran outside and saluted. One of the officers was saying something. At this point all four were standing with their backs to the girls. Just by chance, or deliberately? Eva wondered. She started to have some vague misgivings that she didn't want to put into words. Marie did it for her.

"What the hell's going on?"

Eva was a bit miffed with her. There was no point panicking. Having given voice to their misgivings, they could only get more and more edgy. Marie put her sweater back on, and her short leather anorak, and went outside. Eva followed with a sigh.

"Excuse us," Marie called across to the soldiers. "Can we have a minute of your time?"

Instinctively, Eva expected some saucy response, or at least a knowing grin, but all they got was a single look of dismay. Something really was going on. Marie's voice faltered: she repeated the boys' names and surnames and clasped her hands in a gesture of pleading.

"Can't someone get them for us at last?"

Ultimately it sounded more despairing than reproachful. One of the officers was about to say something, but before he could open his mouth, a Škoda 1203 hearse drew up at the gate. Marie grabbed Eva's arm. The second officer leaned in towards the driver and the guard raised the barrier. The black twelve-O-three continued on in, the soldiers standing aside to let it pass. It passed out of sight among the buildings and the noise of its engine gradually faded away.

"What's happened?" Marie cried.

"Has there been an accident or something?" Eva found her tongue.

She tried to make at least her voice sound calm—as if calm words could temper life's dramas.

"I'm scared," Marie mumbled. "I'm really scared!"

Eva squeezed her hand. All four soldiers were looking away again, or staring down at the asphalt.

"Say something!" Marie screamed.

No response. They fell into each other's arms. Something terrible was going on, something irreparable. In a split second Eva had the following vision: she and Jeff are waiting at a metro station, Jeff is looking troubled, and the sound of an approaching train is coming from the tunnel. Marie began sobbing aloud. 'Let it be Karel,' Eva thought. She felt ashamed of herself, but then repeated the wish with even greater passion: 'Dear God, let it be Karel!'

Suddenly she saw a figure coming running across the open asphalt—it was Jeff. Marie hadn't spotted him yet. For the first time in her life, Eva saw Jeff crying. She knew what it meant, but she also felt hugely, guiltily happy. Jeff's camo suit was unbelievably dirty (the actual source of most of those dark patches would only dawn on Eva later). She wanted to fling herself round his neck, but instantly realised that Jeff had to give Marie a hug first.

161

JEFF

Thick, wet snow was falling and it clung to the soles of his army-issue shoes; the socks he had on were only thin and so he had to keep stamping his feet and wiggling his toes to get at least a bit of warmth. He was worried about seeing Marie and Sebastian, who were fortunately still waiting in the carpark in her parents' car. Better not to think about it. Their other classmates were clustered in little groups; some of the boys were wearing the same suits they'd worn for their teenage dancing classes. There were still fifteen minutes to go; inside, a different service was still going on— the deceased had been seventy-six. Karel twenty-six. Jeff shuffled his feet, a bare paving stone showed beneath his shoe, the white edges of his footprint seeping quickly away. It crossed his mind that Karel would never again make a footprint in the snow. *All that you ever wished for perishes now* it had said on the death notice. There was rather too much pathos to it for his liking, but in essence it was spot-on. Everything was over, irreversibly, irreparably, so where was the point in crocodile consolation. It was pure and utter tragedy, no culmination of a lifetime, nothing of the kind. Just sheer horror. He tried to establish if snowflakes hiss when engulfed by the eternal flame, but he didn't hear anything, despite standing really close. He realised the inappropriateness of his action and turned back to face Eva and Tom. Eva was crying in silence, Tom biting his lips. Now Jeff was feeling more anger than pity. He was chilled to the marrow, quite worn out. It had taken him nine hours to get there from Slovakia and he hadn't slept all night. He couldn't bear to think about it any more. Other things apart, he'd been there when the accident happened; they hadn't. He'd go mad if he kept going back over it. The door of the crematorium opened and the first mourners started to come out.

"Our turn to start hitting the slippery slope," said Tom.

Jeff knew what he meant.

"You've forgotten Irena," he said.

TOM

Eva and Jeff's wedding in October 1989 was the long-deferred good news that they all needed (with the obvious exception of my good self). Belief in happy endings was briefly restored. *Life's not so bad after all*, it might have said on their marriage announcement.

The day before, I'd woken up at five-thirty and my first thought went to Eva: so she's getting married tomorrow. And next week Jeff'll be moving out of *The Den*. Up to that moment I'd been reluctant to admit the impact of the change, but right then it hit home with full force. Life would go on, just the cracks would get a bit wider. I would be staying in that ghastly rented flat with just Skippy for company—Skippy, a gynaecologist who wore cowboy moccasins, listened to country radio and collected chocolate wrappers. Under normal circumstances I'd have tried to get back to sleep, but that time I got up in a manner bordering on the energetic (ahead of us lay Jeff's inevitable stag party), and even went for a shower—like all early-stage alcoholics I enjoyed the illusion of still having a firm grip on life. I shaved and cleaned the sink and the mirror after me; I was pleased with the result, though the contrast with the floor was now so striking that I went and got a broom, bucket and floor cloth. As I bent down busily, my head began to swim and I had to sit down on the wet lino. 'What are you trying to prove, you cretin?' I asked myself as I stared hard at the yellowing bakelite U-bend (we drinkers occasionally talk to ourselves, and not always in the nicest of terms). When Jeff gets up, I mused, and sees that I've tidied up, he'll suspect me of trying to put him off getting married... I stood up, hauled on some clean pants and a vest and went back to my room; I made the bed and aired the place. I crossed to the kitchen, briefly surveyed in horror the dirty glasses, cutlery, encrusted plates and frying pans full of burnt oil—and then quietly washed the lot. Finally I swept and wiped the floor there too. 'Just what are you about, you cretin?'

It still wasn't six-thirty even. I got dressed and went out to get something for breakfast: I bought some rolls, butter, eggs, a few slices of ham, Emmental and smoked salmon and three bottles of Bohemia Sekt. By the time I got back, Skippy was up: loud splashing, throat-clearing and grunting noises were issuing from the bathroom. I desisted from imagining what matinal activities these ghastly sounds were the accompaniment to (or what traces they were leaving on the nice clean floor). I cleared the table of the messy paper containers from a Chinese take-away, the screwed-up napkins and empty wine bottles and spent several long minutes scouring *The Den* for something to wipe the table-top with. In the end I charged into my room, from the plastic basket of clothes ready for ironing I dug out my old, discoloured, somewhat holey, school basketball shirt with its number 13, which I'd been using for years instead of pyjamas, and with a few good yanks tore it into strips. I could feel my heart pounding. So these days, even being unable to find a cloth can get me rattled, I realised.

I went back in the kitchen, wiped the table, put the kettle on the stove and laid the table. From the bathroom came the hiss of a spray, a couple of dull thwacks and a loud snort from Skippy. The door opened a crack and the hallway was invaded by a thin strip of wispy steam—like the creeping sorrow that steals into our misspent lives.

"Early in the morning the maiden gets up, stroking her fanny as she downs her first cup," Skippy recited.

The vast majority of his jingles were marked by the same freakish infantilism: *Is that a girl or a woman, he giggled, lying here ready, so neatly spread-eagled?* Or: *If you look closely at our pet bear, you'll see that his balls are as brown as his hair.* And so on. I didn't even have to look up from my paper for an inkling of Skippy's appearance: the thin, pale chest, the fat belly, and wound round his hips a towel in the colours of this or that football or ice hockey team.

"If I didn't know you were a gynaecologist, I'd have to assume that the bathroom has just witnessed the ablutions of a pig."

In the morning I usually try to avoid conflict, but that day my grand clean-up and the shopping trip made it easier to be frank. Of course Skippy completely passed over my remark—he was more interested in the breakfast spread on the tidy table.

"You been shopping?" he asked, delighted.

"No—this just grew in the night. The mildew about the flat has agreeably mutated."

Skippy missed the point. He succeeded in nicking two slices of ham despite my lashing at him with my fork.

"Shouldn't we wait for Jeff?" I challenged him. "You can go and wake him."

Skippy took two steps and hammered at the door of *No. 1.*

"Wakey, wakey!" he bellowed in a lousy imitation of a sergeant major. "Rise and shine!"

He grinned cheerily at me. He was twenty-seven with a hairline more receding than Jack Nicholson's. It wasn't the first time I realised that I was actually sorry for him.

"Do go and get dressed, Skippy, for God's sake," I said with a sigh.

"Make me some ham and eggs, will you? I won't be having the salmon. The colour of it reminds me too much of a vaginal mucous membrane."

He bent forward and sniffed at the plate.

"And if I'm honest, not just the colour..." he giggled and clapped one hand to his mouth.

If I were a woman, I thought, I should be particularly careful about my choice of gynaecologist.

Jeff came in and surveyed the table in surprise. He was stripped to the waist and looked like a man in an aftershave commercial. I imagined Eva clinging to him the following night, and handed him a glass of bubbly.

"You're crazy!" he said with a shake of his head. "I can't start drinking at seven in the morning. I'm getting married tomorrow."

"Quite the reverse," said Skippy, smiling. "You're getting married tomorrow, so today you *have* to start drinking first thing."

"A toast, then," I suggested. "I say, Skippy, try thinking of something at least slightly romantic. Something less stupid than your usual efforts. Something to match the historic significance of the day and make it that little extra bit special. Why else do you suppose, you arch-pricks, that I was hard at it cleaning the flat at six this morning?"

Jeff finally noticed the tidy kitchen surfaces and sparkling floor.

"Wow!"

"Come on, Skippy, are you going to propose that damn toast then?"

Skippy raised his glass and looked each of us straight in the eye.

"So skirts up!" he cried and burst into a giggle.

On Saturday I woke at nine in Žaneta's bed-sit in Modřany, quite incapable of recalling how and when I'd got there. For a few seconds I nearly panicked, but then I spotted my wallet, keys and ID card on a chair under my crumpled jeans; the legs of the latter were completely inside out. What a battlefield must look like, was what crossed my mind. I laughed aloud, which meant one thing: I was still drunk. I could hear Žaneta clomping around in the bathroom: one sound told me she was opening some kind of cream. Liposomes penetrate the deepest layers of her skin, making it clearer and brighter. I cautiously tried to sit on the bed: my stomach seemed to be all right. Obviously I had a headache, but mercifully not nearly as bad as might have been expected after some twenty hours of boozing. I tried to reconstruct the previous day and night: we'd taken in about eight or nine different pubs and bars; I recalled Jeff and

Skippy leaving the last one even before midnight struck, whereas I (alone with my misery) had gone on to the Barrel wine bar, where I—God in Heaven, yes—joined two young couples from Pilsen. They gladly made room for me at their table and I repaid them by arrogantly refusing to engage in any other topic but Eva. Here the film of my memories sort of came to an end. To be continued. I went over to the bathroom, still wearing a smile. Žaneta looked at me with distrust.

"Good morning. It was so wonderful last night, darling," I said. "I suggest the following agenda: first I'll clean my teeth, then I'll give you a kiss."

"Good try, except you weren't here last night," she put me in my place. "You were driven here at six in the morning by some folk from Brno. You fell asleep before I'd even got your shoes off."

Something here didn't fit, but why bother with details on such a special day?

"Aha, the good folk of Brno understand me."

"They didn't look as if they understood you. They looked annoyed."

"A disagreement among friends," I replied with a shrug.

I began cleaning my teeth: I had to focus a bit so as to get the brush into my mouth at the first go—and obviously I was careful not to push it too far back. My movements were about a third of their usual speed, while Žaneta's were faster. She was just trying to do up the zip of her cocktail dress, which—as we could both see—was too tight on her.

"Do get a move on!" she snapped.

She was a film production manager; the year before she'd had an ever so slight promotion, so for the first time in her life she had four subordinates to boss around. I looked at her and drew a callous mental comparison of her with Eva.

"Why?" I asked. I was entering *phase one of the bullishness of inebriates*.

"In case you've forgotten, you're to be a witness at this wedding lark. So even in your present condition you must realise that you've got to be there."

"And do you know what my being a witness there bears witness to?"

She withdrew the lipstick from her lips and sighed.

"To the fact that you're Jeff's best friend," she said, adopting a more conciliatory tone.

"To my cowardice."

She waved this away: it wasn't something she cared to hear. As if what she already knew wasn't enough. She'd wanted to live with *a young poet*, and instead, twice a week, she'd got this almost thirty-year-old alcoholic in her bed-sit. Instead of sharing intimacies in verse with eternity, I was using her as an eternal surrogate. A *body double*: doubling for Eva in the bedroom scenes. I laughed again.

"You've got ten minutes to pull yourself together," Žaneta advised me resolutely.

She was standing behind me, make-up on and sorrowful. There was a time when she'd hoped that I was Mr Right, but by now she knew I was merely the *fourth serious* relationship in her life. She still slept with me, but out of inertia, and when on Friday evenings she went into town with her girlfriends she would invariably come alive with renewed hope. Her grey-green eyes were already looking for number five. I put my arms round her; at first she resisted, but then yielded.

"Understand that it's going to be hard for me too," she whispered.

JEFF

Wherever he and Eva went after they were married—visiting friends, to the cottage in the country, on a holiday by the sea—they were always there. Her *little suitors*. That's what she called them. They were aged mostly between five and ten. On first seeing her, they would gape at her open-mouthed—and within two minutes they'd be head over heels in love with her. After which they'd never leave her side. They'd demand crayons then draw for her their very best pictures ever. If Eva had to go to the toilet, they'd go with her and wait devotedly outside the door.

"At least I hope they did," Jeff would say acerbically.

Every time they went out, they'd seize Eva's hand and not let go of it. They'd push Jeff aside and deliberately get under his feet. If he tried to tell Eva something, they'd keep interrupting. If he was about to cream Eva on the beach, they'd grab the tube from his hand and do it themselves. And if he was finally going to make love with her, he'd find that Sebastian was already there, sleeping in his spot. Formally, Jeff might indeed be Eva's husband, but at such moments that counted for nothing: now she was only Sebastian's. Next time it would be young Richard or little Pavel. Or some other little brat.

With the feigned, sneaky innocence of children, they would snuggle up to his wife, sit on her lap, rest their heads on her breasts and even *kiss* her. Their parents, grandmas, uncles and other relatives thought it rather sweet; Jeff found it *tasteless*. Outwardly he would smile with the others, but in his heart of hearts he hated the little bastards—as they did him. They refused to go mushrooming unless *Auntie Eva* went as well. They refused to go skiing unless *Auntie Eva* joined them on the chair lift. They refused to go to bed until *Auntie Eva* read them a story. They'd have fits of hysteria if they couldn't sit next to her, and Jeff had to give up his place.

"They're common-or-garden emotional blackmailers!" he insisted to Eva as they got changed in their room having come back from the piste. "Can't people see it? I don't understand why you all put up with it."

Yet again someone came knocking on the door: another metre-high suitor was standing in the corridor. Jeff stood firmly in the doorway.

"Will Auntie Eva come and play snap with us?"

The lad tried to see inside; Jeff had to push him away.

"Definitely not," he said, unsmiling. "*Auntie Eva* can't stand snap. Playing snap makes *Auntie Eva* feel sick."

"You're lying!"

The little weasel slipped between his legs, ran into the room and leapt into the half-naked Eva's arms.

Eva laughed.

EVA

In the late 1980s she garnered from Skippy and two other doctors sundry information about alternative birthing options. Of course, she'd want a water birth, but when she told her gynaecologist so in February 1990, he looked at her as benignly as if she'd just voiced a desire to give birth in the heap of filthy snow beneath his surgery window.

"I should remind you that man is a mammal," he said with a disagreeable smile. "Your baby will definitely not have gills…"

She knew that the doctor was prejudiced but lacked the courage to fight back.

In defiance of all the assurances that first-timers often *go beyond their due date*, her labour pains started in the late afternoon of June 29—three weeks early. She wasn't quite sure that it was the real thing, but she wanted to play safe. She packed and ordered a cab. Jeff was in London on a two-day business trip; she couldn't hold that against him: he wasn't to know. When she called her parents, she got the answering machine. Finally she phoned *The Den*.

"Hi," Tom greeted her in surprise. "Jeff's not here."

"I know."

Somewhat at length she explained her predicament.

"I'll go with you," Tom broke in. "I'll be there in ten minutes."

He made it in the nick of time: more contractions started just as she was leaving the house. Tom had to support her with both hands. The taxi driver was standing outside his cab having a smoke.

"Oh dear!" he exclaimed the moment he saw her. "Oh dear!"

"Podolí," Tom instructed him. "Podolí maternity hospital."

"Just stay calm," the taxi driver begged, initially taking Tom to be a random by-passer.

He tossed his cigarette, sat behind the wheel and turned the key. Tom opened a rear door and helped Eva inside. The cabbie watched them in his rear-view mirror, beneath which dangled a little Rubik's Cube. Eva tried to focus on its colours: red, green, yellow, blue.

"You okay, Ma'am?"

"Absolutely."

Tom quickly ran round the car and got in next to her. The pains eased.

"At least Daddy hasn't fainted yet," the driver joked.

"This isn't exactly the daddy," said Eva.

"My mistake, sorry."

They were driving along Tábor Street. Eva smiled at Tom and held his hand. She sensed something rising unstoppably within him—his eyes were moist.

"Just stay calm!" the driver repeated into his mirror.

Tom had to keep clearing his throat as he tried to maintain his self-control.

"I'm sorry," he whispered to her. "Sorry."

They descended from Pankrác to the embankment: now she could see the river and the boats at anchor—as ever, the sight of water helped her relax. On the pavement outside the hospital entrance she spotted Skippy, waving at them, and she started to laugh.

"God almighty!" Tom sighed.

Skippy was running alongside the car, banging on the bonnet.

"This one isn't the daddy either," Eva informed the taxi driver, "but you can stop for him anyway."

The driver braked, Skippy opened the passenger side door and got in; he immediately turned to Eva and took her left hand in his (her right hand was still being held by Tom).

"Darling! Sweetie!" he moaned. "Are you okay?"

The driver looked on disapprovingly.

173

Although it passed without complications, the birth took almost eleven hours. As Eva was being moved early next morning from the labour ward, she, with no idea why, found herself counting the fluorescent tubes on the ceiling: three, four, five... She recognised her own ward, came to her senses and started asking for Alice, but before the porter could reply, an elderly lady doctor came up bearing Alice in her arms. The baby was asleep, her fine hair stuck together with dried blood.

"Perfectly healthy," said the doctor, smiling.

Eva shifted sideways to make room for Alice beside her in the bed and covered her up. She couldn't keep her eyes off her. The doctor pointed to the metal side table on which stood a little plastic bucket full of roses.

"I presume this was brought by your father."

Eva tore open the attached envelope and raised an eyebrow.

"It wasn't my father," she said. "It was my Czech teacher."

SKIPPY

I've seen one of my patients five times this month already. No sooner had I dealt with her persistent vaginal discharge when some warts appeared. In addition to that she's had her car stolen and her cousin *went missing* a fortnight ago—and March, according to one horoscope, as she told me, was to be a month of joy. Instead of giving these so-called astrologists a damn good hiding, we sneak peaks at their outpourings in even the most widely read dailies... The world's a crazy place.

I'm not bothered by STDs, at least I get to see what I'm spared till the day I die, tee-hee. I like doing ultrasound best. If everything's okay, it's a nice job. Sometimes a new dad will look in. We sit there, the three of us, the other two holding hands, I just witter on and think to myself: life ain't bad. It's like roulette—none of us can ever know what number our little ball will land on. Not even this six-month-old embryo that's just sucking its thumb. The first time I saw it, while I was still a student, I got all tearful, just like the mums. Now, though, the novelty's worn off, as it's bound to with anybody, but I'd like a kid of my own, so badly that I could cry. Three and a half kilos of pure happiness, that's what Jeff told me after Alice was born. An' I believe him. My own biological clock has been marking the hours, and years now, like the astronomical clock on Old Town Square. Except, how to come by a baby without stealing? *Shto dyelat*? as our Russian teacher used to say. Nothing, take things as they are. In every raffle someone wins the dinner for two, and someone has to make do with the pot of marmalade. That's life, and it's silly to make a fuss of it.

JEFF

For as long as he and Eva had been together he would shower twice a day, sometimes three times.

"You stink, sporty," she would tell him.

Whenever he came in from a bike ride, he would toss his sweat-soaked shirt straight in the washer so that Eva didn't have to touch it. He stripped, loaded any other dirty washing, selected the programme, switched it on and went for a shower. Having left the bathroom, he usually found that Eva had opened a window to give the flat an airing.

He shaved every morning, but if he wanted them to make love, he had to shave in the evening as well.

"You're all scratchy," she would say if he didn't, and simply turn her back on him.

A bit miffed, Jeff would stare into the darkness and run a finger over his budding whiskers. His father and mother used to cut each other's toenails and slough the hardened skin from each other's heels with a pumice stone; and of course they washed each other's backs. Eva would lock herself in the bathroom. Jeff could never understand why.

"If there's something you don't understand, just ask," his father used to tell him when he was at university.

In the course of his marriage to Eva he had learned that some things are best left unknown.

After the divorce he started visiting a certain nightclub, roughly twice a month (on the first occasion he'd been taken there by an older colleague from work). With at least six or eight girls on hand, he could always pick and choose—though at first he only ever went upstairs with Edita. Their evening hour grew ever more cosy—Jeff didn't need to shower any more, let alone shave. Edita told him about her family: her father was passionate about making model aeroplanes. She'd had a go herself, just to please him, but as she took a razor blade to *a balsa-wood spar* she almost cut her finger off—so she gave up. Her dad had wanted a boy, but the poor guy got three girls. He, her mum and her sisters had a fair idea of what she did for a living, but pretended not to know. She'd trained as a seamstress. She couldn't buy them any presents. If she did get them a microwave or deep fat fryer, her dad wouldn't even unpack it—or if he did, he'd just look inside the box to check it wasn't some disgusting gadget from a sex-shop. The ever-increasing familiarity began to bother Jeff. As he turned up one evening and Edita leapt onto his lap as usual, he gently removed her, adding that this time he'd rather have one of the others. Edita looked aggrieved, which he thought rather comical in a prostitute.

"I can't help it, sugar," he said. "It's how we men are made. That's life."

He never called anyone *sugar*, but in a whorehouse it didn't matter. In a whorehouse hardly anything mattered— and that suited him just nicely.

"Life's a bitch," Edita said in a whisper.

"I'm afraid I half-agree with you there."

He'd never have admitted it, but he knew there were times when he imitated Tom's way of speaking, including his diction.

But once in while he did go with Edita.

"Shall I run the bath?" she asked him, eager to please.

Jeff nodded. He got undressed, while Edita studied him.

"Why do you actually come here? We both know that there outside—" with a wet arm she pointed to the window concealed behind its burgundy roller-blind, "you of all people could get any of this for absolutely nothing."

If there's something you don't understand, he thought, don't ask.

TOM

I appreciate that history does sometimes repeat itself, but in this case the coincidence was more than striking; it raised the suspicion that history (notably my own) is a moody creature endowed with a capacity for schadenfreude: in June 1992 I was standing in for a sick colleague and taking Klára's class for a Czech lesson.

I turned up in a mood to match the realisation that I'd just lost my sole free period of the day (originally I'd meant to spend it over a coffee and the literary weekly)—but suddenly I spotted her: she was in the second row, by the window, and, like the others, she was watching me with a degree of curiosity (the explanation was simple: I was only thirty, I hadn't taught their class before, and, last but not least, I had the reputation of a twice-*published* poet). In the first instant I felt I'd fallen victim to one of Skippy's jokes: the same mouth, the same smooth forehead and the fair down at her temples. Watching me was Eva.

Even back then I was aware of the measure of obsessiveness of my yearnings, but did nothing to temper it. My long-standing obsession was as stupid as it was sublime—it depends how you look at it. *Steep* your life in unfulfilled longing, or *squander* it. I'm not clear myself: sometimes I think I'm a tragic hero, other times (more often) a character out of the sixth series of a once successful comedy for teenagers. The latter is most likely right. Today I know that, but since that time I've passed forty. Diagnosis: belated regret. It can't be helped now. Either I'll have to kill myself (which I can't do), or carry on as before. *She was connected to him through a tacit adolescent agreement*, I read recently in a novel by Zadie Smith. Somehow I'll get through the few years left to me before I drink myself to death.

I managed to stay calm—but then I had a full forty-five minutes ahead of me. I took the register and quasi-casually asked someone what they'd been doing last. Interwar verse? Right-ho, let's get to it. It was enough to dust off my old armoury and quote them anything that I still remembered by heart. Halas, Seifert, Biebl, Nezval, obviously. Some juicy details from those great lives. Know when to make them laugh and when to be serious. Be both boyishly playful and manfully sombre. Call a spade a spade. Not lie.

All those *tricks*. All that *dishonesty*.

"What *did* you do with them last week?" their regular teacher asked me later. "They were in raptures."

I felt as if she'd caught me masturbating.

"The regular stuff," I replied with a shrug.

"Next time I'd be grateful for a bit more fatigue, apathy and lack of interest," the rather nice colleague said with a smile. "Otherwise you'll upset our norms."

"Will do."

"Oh and before I forget: Klára—the pretty blonde—asks if you'd set up a literature club for them after the holidays."

So another summer break to get through—I'd been there before. Another hot and stuffy August in Prague. In deserted, air-conditioned shops I bought a supply of jeans, black T-shirts and some proper shirts, but *casual*.

Then from September onwards I saw her every week: for a whole hour I had her to myself. My twelve-years-younger rivals (instantly identifiable among the other pupils) were easy to disarm: by ingratiating myself with them. I lent them books worth reading, showed them seriously good films, and read the tripe they wrote themselves. I was suitably critical (I didn't want to blow my cover), but could give praise where praise was due. *You've worked this paragraph out nicely, Petr. It's actually brilliant—and you know that 'brilliant' isn't a word I bandy about lightly...* I watched how Klára thawed, how she grew more responsive by the week, how she gradually fell in love with me (I'd loved her for years by then), but besides a sense of hesitant elation, there was also a slight feeling of disgust, the disgust of my *civilian* self, you might say: a disgust with myself, with literature, with girls.

JEFF

When Tom first introduced Jeff to Klára (they'd happened to bump into each other on one of the local squares), her appearance so reminded the latter of Eva that it almost took his breath away—but he pretended not to have noticed.

"Let me introduce you—though we haven't got much time. Klára still has some biology homework to do," Tom joked ineptly.

Jeff felt as if he'd sunk back through time. Klára blushed.

"I finished school last month," she said shyly in her defence, as if having the school-leaving exams behind her could change anything: she was still exactly thirteen years younger than Eva.

The resemblance was staggering. Such difference as there was, Jeff thought, was like when certain car-owners switch the badge on their car for another: what you're standing in front of is obviously a Škoda Favorit, but the blue enamel oval screwed into the radiator is trying to kid you into thinking it's a Ford.

"Next weekend, I'm going to meet her parents formally," Tom said, smiling, with one arm round Klára's shoulders. "I say 'formally' because they already know me from parent-teacher evenings."

When Jeff reported the encounter to Eva, she found it hugely amusing. He hadn't been able to make her laugh so much in ages, so he was glad they'd found some common ground for once. He opened a bottle of red and they spent the evening picking over that relationship with its great discrepancy of age. Jeff was of the view that for Tom—consciously or otherwise—Klára was just a surrogate for something he'd missed out on in his youth.

"And what did he miss out on in his youth?" Eva said with a smile. "What *can* you be thinking of?"

Jeff knew that Eva wanted it put into words.

"You. As we all well know. Klára's his compensation for having been turned down by you."

"But that's not true," Eva said, satisfied. "There was nothing to turn down, because he never once told me he loved me, as was alleged."

"But everybody knew."

Eva leant against his shoulder. She took a sip of wine and half-closed her eyes. Then she added languidly that it was Tom's problem, for which she couldn't feel in the least responsible.

"But it's still an embarrassment," Jeff concluded staunchly.

"Somewhat pubertal," Eva agreed. "It's time he grew up."

That evening they had sex for the first time in three weeks.

TOADY

Tom drew me to him and kissed me on the cheek as if it were the most natural thing in the world.

This is how it came about: that evening, Boris had popped out to the Bareta place for two olive and camembert pizzas and he'd run into Tom. Tom recognised him, which was surprising since they'd only ever met once before, at our wedding. Tom had been sitting alone, probably in need of company, because he immediately ordered a bottle of white; when they'd finished it, Boris invited him to ours (from my reminiscences he'd known for a long time what Tom had once meant to me and he wanted to make my day).

"Hi there, my girl," said Tom.

Unlike Skippy and the others he never used my nickname—thereby also raising false hopes in me of course. Not that I was so naïve back then as to hope that this nice, clever boy would fall in love with me of all people, but... All right, I can't tell a lie: of course I *was* that daft! If you believe that *plain* teenage girls don't have dreams, then you're wrong. They do, but they keep them very much to themselves because they know full well they'd make themselves look ridiculous (it did occur to me once that if Tom had treated me with the same more or less well disguised callousness as everybody else, it might have been better and given me a sounder grip on reality...).

We shared the two pizzas between us and drank three bottles of wine. I rose to fetch another from the kitchen. While I was looking for the corkscrew, I caught the sound of Tom yawning and trying to suppress the yawn—in my husband's presence people were frequently given to suppressing yawns.

"By the way," Boris called to me, "have you heard?"

I got three plates out and started preparing a *modest midnight collation* (in Tom's presence my language can sometimes get a bit flowery). I was in just the right mood to smack the light switch with my whole palm as if it weren't a little square of hard plastic, but the backside of a young toreador (I've never been to a bullfight, but I've always had a weakness for toreadors). I squinted against the purring fluorescent tube—I can't abide their cold light, but being drunk made it tolerable—and I gaily kicked out of sight under the kitchen units every pickled onion that fell on the floor. "Let them rot!" I said almost audibly, refusing to admit that next morning I'd be down on all fours poking at the onions with a broom handle as if they were billiard balls. But at that moment I didn't care. I opened our technologically mediaeval fridge, took out some ham off the bone, pressed it to my bosom and gave it a cuddle. It seemed like the most wondrous ham off the bone that I'd ever seen. The world was a marvellous place to be. There, in *my very own* living room—a mere three metres from the bedroom—sat Tom!

"Hey there!" Boris hollered again. "I asked you, have you heard?"

"No. What?" I called back—and then it suddenly dawned.

I set the ham down on the draining board, rested both hands on the edge and waited.

"That I'm getting married the day after tomorrow," bellowed Tom.

I heard him clink glasses with Boris. I forced myself to return from the kitchen and to *blithely* raise an ugly eyebrow.

"You, *getting married*? That's got to be love and a half…"

They may both have feared how I might react (otherwise why had they been so backward in coming forward with such vital news?), but now they seemed happy.

"It is," said Tom laboriously. "She's… she's so… beautiful!"

He closed his lovely eyes, which meant I could go back to the ham off the bone and quietly cry my own eyes out.

TOM

In the morning, in the bathroom, I was suddenly struck by something: I was freshly shaven (a wedding's a wedding) and the mirror was clean. The basin likewise. I looked around me: the bathroom had been tidied. History was repeating itself.

I entered the kitchen and found the table set for three—that probably meant that Jeff would also be joining us for breakfast. Skippy was standing by the cooker making me some ham and eggs.

"Unbelievable," I remarked.

Skippy grinned with pride, then took a bottle of Finnish vodka out of the freezer.

"Thanks for the breakfast, Skippy, but I really won't have any vodka," I resisted. "For one thing, I'm getting married tomorrow morning, and for another I already got drunk last night."

"One shouldn't confine oneself to speaking in banalities. All you say is so predictable... Why don't you try to be at least a tiny bit original once in a while?"

This was almost identical to the kind of things I'd say to him.

"Okay, here's something that may surprise you: last night I got drunk with Toady and her husband."

"Get away! You got drunk with her?" Skippy was truly amazed. "How so?"

"Pure chance."

"Why would anyone get drunk in the company of a woman who looks like a mother jackal?"

'Why would anyone get drunk every other day with someone who looks like a penguin and calls himself Skippy, as if he was a kangaroo?' I mused in turn.

"Christ, Skippy... Where do you get your metaphors from?"

"Good though, eh?"

"Hm, I'm not so sure. Not knowing what a *mother jackal* looks like..."

"Pretty stupid," Skippy laughed. "Like Toady."

This was going nowhere. Skippy poured vodkas all round and I shook my head resolutely.

"You're getting married tomorrow, but *not till midday*," he reminded me. "Incidentally, shouldn't I give the bride a once-over?"

"I wouldn't trust you with her, even if she was bleeding profusely."

"You wouldn't?" Skippy enquired ingenuously. "Whyever not?"

"You wouldn't understand."

In resignation I grabbed a glass and started thinking about a toast.

"So, skirts up!" Skippy cried.

I'd known him since primary school and was convinced that at least a section of the roots of his being defeated in life (if such a division of roots isn't debatable and if one accepts that there is such a thing in human life as a victory) led back to his first brilliant bit of tomfoolery: at the age of ten, in the school dinner hall, he had stripped to the waist, lain down on a table where some older girls were sitting, tipped two bowls of blancmange onto his chest and started wiggling in just the right way—and that took some courage! Carry that off and you have to become the school freak, and in the following weeks and months they'll be queuing up to see you... Skippy had been paying the price of that success ever since. A victim of self-stylisation. Buried alive at the age of thirty beneath a mound of schoolboy pranks. Come to think of it, I mused, the worst thing about adolescence isn't acne, sexual deprivation or all the usual embarrassments; no, worst of all is that, for all the utter confusion and helplessness, everybody keeps up a *veneer of normality*. The most terrible thing about puberty is that pretence of being *blasé*. I see it at school every day. Sometimes I wouldn't mind telling my students: Just try and imagine for once that we adults can see right through you. We can see how foolish and insecure you are, you know—so why, for God's sake, do you play at being so *cool*? Why, you hopeless dummies, do you keep saying things are *cool*—even after you've, say, just been cheated out of the love of your life?

186

JEFF

It was 10 a.m.—and they'd got through over half that bottle of vodka. Although Jeff tried to eat plenty after each glass, he could tell he was slightly drunk. 'Even breakfast with Tom and Skippy means boozing,' he thought with some irritation. If the choice were his, he'd much rather have gone for a bike ride. A gentle climb over many long kilometres, along a narrow country lane lined on both sides with apple trees— that would do just nicely. With shrivelled apples on the bare branches and hoarfrost on the grass. He started to look forward to getting his bike out on Sunday and riding out to Vrchlabí.

"I've always thought," said Tom, savouring the occasion, "that a drink first thing in the morning has something to be said for it. In the evening I'm so knackered that alcohol often gets the better of me, but up until lunchtime I'm generally as fresh as a daisy and a match for anyone."

Skippy glanced at Jeff and smirked:

"He's talking like a book again. A sure sign that he's plastered!"

"That is somewhat inaccurate," Tom objected. "As I've just explained, up until lunchtime I can be tipsy *and* alert *at one and the same time*. Have you ever seen plaster being alert?"

Jeff had stopped listening—when he wanted to, he could switch off completely. Tom's blathering got on his nerves. Back when Tom was seventeen, Vartecký had praised him for his *surprisingly rich vocabulary*—'...and that's kept him going till thirty,' Jeff thought. Sometimes he saw Tom as a little boy with a new bike, riding round the houses all day

187

long to make sure that everyone's seen—after a time it had become unseemly.

"And d'you know what's worst?" Tom asked Skippy. "I've barely got myself sorted out after thirty, barely got used to undone buttons and lots of cleavage," he repeated for Jeff's benefit, having noticed that he'd looked up, "and along come these *skimpy tops*."

He made a pregnant pause.

"And with them bare midriffs. The intimacy of the belly-button revealed. And sometimes those two dimples above the buttocks."

"Oh my god, buttocks! Glorious, firm little buttocks!" Skippy exclaimed.

"And when a top is really skimpy and flaps outwards properly, there's also that new, unprecedently exciting view of breasts *from below*."

Skippy bit into his forefinger.

"Breasts from below?" Jeff queried. "You'd have to be kneeling, wouldn't you?"

Tom ignored him.

"And after all the trouble getting used to this as well, after you've barely achieved a measure of constraint so that, faced with these erotic sophistications—"

"You can keep your bladder under control?" Jeff broke in caustically.

"—you can at least preserve a minimum of human dignity, along come *hip-huggers*."

"I love hip-huggers!" Skippy yelped.

"With the *knickers* peeping out. Brazen, vulgar, risqué panties, the *acknowledgement* of their presence a sheer provocation. What was once the prerogative of one man's eyes is now there for all to see—that's the brutal essence of this fashion. Several times a day *each* of us can enjoy the status of the elect—but with none of the critical privileges. We can see, but we mustn't touch. Lace trim is a portent of pleasures that are not to be."

"Nice one!" cried Skippy the way he did when he was young. Tom was obviously quite pleased with himself.

"Klára doesn't wear hip-huggers?" Jeff asked.

"She even wore them to school—how do you think she snared me?"

After a moment's indecision Jeff clinked glasses with him. "Here's hoping it'll work out for you."

"To the bride and groom!" Skippy shouted.

"And now I'm going to ask *you* something," Tom said to Jeff, having set his glass down. "I've been meaning to for a long time: Did she, or didn't she sleep with Vartecký?"

Even after all the years that had passed since, the question immediately created tension. Tom apparently enjoyed picking over the past—Jeff certainly didn't share his keenness.

"I hope you don't mind me asking."

Jeff remained silent.

"What's the problem?" Skippy failed to understand. "You're getting divorced, aren't you?"

"It sometimes strikes me," Jeff began, "that you two will still be fussing about Eva and Vartecký in retirement. Though he'll be dead by then."

"Both those things are highly probable," said Tom. "But you haven't answered the question."

Jeff took a drink, to gain time. He knew now that he'd tell Tom, although he sensed there was some schadenfreude in his asking, something almost vengeful.

"She did."

"I guessed as much," Tom responded with a nod, before overriding the utterance with several shakes of his head.

"They carried on for years."

"*Years?!*"

Tom sank his head in his hands. Jeff and Skippy exchanged glances.

"What's up?" said Skippy. "It's ancient history."

"The bitch," Tom muttered. "The damned bitch!"

TOADY

We ugly folk find others not only better-looking, but also more confident, clever, even-tempered and generally happier—and, more often than not, we're shocked when we learn otherwise. So for example, when Eva first saw Klára at Tom's wedding, she immediately withdrew into herself. I wasn't the only one to notice. Several times Jeff asked her something, but she didn't once reply. Her only communication was with little Alice. Me and some of the other girls went over to say hello, but above all to see her reaction to the unholy likeness between herself and Klára.

"So what do you reckon?" Zuzana whispered, looking sidelong at the young bride.

"Nothing."

"I didn't know you had a younger sister..."

"Ha ha."

Even Klára herself was visibly unsettled by Eva and kept turning her back on her. To me it was like when two women turn up at a party wearing the same outfit.

"She's pretty, true enough," I said, "but there's one key thing she lacks."

"And what's that?" Eva asked cautiously.

"Your d.o.b."

She patted me gratefully.

Marie arrived half an hour late (the ceremony was over and Klára and Tom were having their photographs taken). There were dark circles in the armpits of her yellow dress. The lady who was babysitting Sebastian had been stuck in a traffic jam, she explained apologetically. She gave us all a hug—me first, would you believe! She never stopped smiling and had plenty to say: she was teaching infants, played at *Winnie the Pooh* with the kids, and she'd started going to yoga classes. There was even *a new man* in her life, but for now she was keeping him *at arm's length*.

"Blokes are terribly inconsiderate," she said, pulling a face, "first they put you up the duff, then they blithely get themselves run over by an armoured personnel carrier..."

We were moved to silence.

"And you two, you're okay, I trust?" she said turning to Jeff and Eva.

"Sure," Jeff said after a slight pause. "We're cool."

Eva just shrugged. We all saw it.

"If it's not a life that's at stake, then there's bugger-all at stake," said Marie.

TOM

The radio was on, playing some typically inane song—and Klára raised the volume with the remote. Somewhat annoyed,

I looked up from my mid-term essays, but she didn't even notice: she was lying with her back to me on our *Karlanda* sofa, reading *Elle* and lightly tapping her lips with the silver tip of her ballpoint. Then I registered that her lips were moving. There could be no doubt: she knew the stupid lyrics by heart.

The furnishings of our bed-sit were the product of a triple compromise: first we'd had to coordinate Klára's ideas (IKEA with the grafted-on sentimentality of little girls' rooms) with mine (originality, minimalism, utility), then match the outcome to our finances, and finally, out of politeness, to a number of studies provided by Toady, who'd done them entirely free of charge in light of our friendship of many years' standing (as she put it somewhat grandly).

"I must tell you in advance: I find tasteful accommodation boring," I'd warned her, in allusion to Heinrich Böll.

"Well," she'd said bluntly, having inspected the full-colour sketches Klára had produced on graph paper, "if you leave the furnishing to her, you certainly won't be bored."

For the last year we'd both been pretty bored (me, in close contact with a thing of beauty—yet being bored; I'd never have believed it possible). We even admitted it: we would jointly ruminate aloud on who we might invite over for the evening. If we left the flat to go out for the evening, things weren't much better. Most people of Klára's age got on my nerves, and my friends got on hers: I promised her a well-educated, amusing young journalist—only for us to spend the entire evening in the company of a bald thirty-something who either talked of nothing but himself or tested her on her knowledge of literature. And so on. Literature had lost its allure long before. She was into things that were of supreme indifference to me: dance music, roller skates, computer graphics, snowboarding outfits. She would appeal, with justification, to her very youth—and I would feel offended. I drank and I taught her to drink; drunkenness exposed her wild side: in bed, her willingness to do absolute anything I asked of her in a fit of lust came as a shock. I began to realise that sooner or later she'd start cheating on me. We cooked, we put on weight, we exercised. We contemplated three-way and four-way sex and had fits of jealousy as it transpired we weren't the first to think of it. We lied to each other. We told each other the truth. We cheated on each other. We repeatedly considered separation, separated and made up. In the end—as we'd both long anticipated—we parted for good.

SKIPPY

Plane tickets are getting unbelievably cheap; I did a random search on the internet yesterday: Paris three thousand crowns, London two thousand five hundred. So it's not the least surprising that whole hoards of drunken Brits keep coming over, as if on the tram, not by plane. Melbourne twelve thou. Ten years ago Australia cost thirty. Last month Claude wrote to me saying I was getting scared even of gays from Australia because, now plane tickets cost next to nothing, they might seriously show up. Up to now they'd been safely *across the ocean* and that was that, but today even your ordinary Melbourne librarian could fly hither and yon and that was making me nervous. Without thinking twice, I wrote back saying why didn't he come then; I'd be waiting for him at arrivals with five tea roses—and in the next three urgent emails I went back on it. The image of him packing a heap of brand new Y-fronts scared the living daylights out of me. Of course that made him mad and he wrote back suggesting I find myself a Martian: now they'd found water on Mars, there might even be the odd homosexual there—but there'd be no danger of him flying down to see me in a hurry. '*Fuck you!*' I tapped back. 'You wouldn't know how,' he wrote straight back. The truth is, I keep playing at being someone else. At school I played the class buffoon, in the surgery I try to mimic those ever-so-polite doctors you see in American films, and when I'm with Jeff and Tom I play at male sexuality: I don't do the shopping, I never tidy up and I'm foul-mouthed. Tee-hee. Obviously I'm no actor, so I often overdo it and act out of character, but do you suppose those two idiots have ever once noticed? They're so dense they even try to help me pick up girls. I don't know what I'd have to do for it to get through to them after twenty-five years. I suppose the only way would be to tell them. But that's the one thing I can't do: after a quarter of a century of laughing at jokes about poofters—or even telling them yourself—you can hardly announce that, by the way, you're also, actually, gay. 'Incidentally, Jeff, did I ever tell you I'm a poof?' I just can't imagine it. Some admissions may be held back a little while, but twenty-five years strikes me as a bit long. So my only option is to plough gaily on, but the way things are going and if plane tickets get so ridiculously cheaper and cheaper, one day Claude's going to turn up unannounced and then I'll have to go right out and buy some tight leather trousers and a pink shirt. And I can thank my lucky arse that back in primary school I hadn't started a penfriendship with someone from the Soviet Union—otherwise instead of a librarian from Melbourne I could end up with a nancy boy steelworker from the Kuzbass and they'd have to carry Jeff out on a stretcher.

JEFF

After the divorce Jeff had Alice for one afternoon a week and every other weekend. Most times they'd go to the swimming baths or the pictures. They'd spend almost all the weekends away from Prague: skiing in winter, camping or cycling in the summer. Today, if Jeff asks Alice about all those outings in retrospect, he's disappointed to discover that she hardly remembers any of them. 'Whatever, maybe it was worth it anyway,' he consoles himself.

What Alice does remember is the way Skippy used to lark about: he started going away with them and was even prepared to miss major football or ice hockey matches. Right at the outset Jeff had been emphatic that Skippy should not use foul language in Alice's hearing, and Skippy, to his amazement, did indeed refrain. The rest of his behaviour, however, was even more childish than usual (little Alice's presence serving as his alibi): outside he would commit all manner of breaches of good conduct, leap about, pull funny faces and make up silly jingles just for Alice's benefit, like *Keep digging that hole, the vicar cried / But what on earth for? An elephant's died.* Rhymes like that would then go round and round in Jeff's head for weeks on end, but his daughter was thrilled—and that was the main thing.

A few years later Tom started coming with them too.

He also was quick to endear Alice to him: he'd discovered that she loved ghost stories, so he started telling her idiosyncratic versions of various horror films (Jeff had to rein him in a bit so Alice could get to sleep). The good thing was that during their shared weekends he drank a lot less, with the result that his exhibitionistic loquacity was reduced to an acceptable minimum.

Jeff was convinced that, as Alice grew, she reminded Tom more and more of Eva. At any rate, he often caught him watching her discreetly.

"Is there anything in the world more *exquisite* than that?" he asked Jeff one evening during a boating weekend on the Sázava.

His eyes indicated Alice, who was sitting a little way off, gazing absently into the campfire. She was wearing Jeff's black sweatshirt, which was so big on her that she could hunch both legs inside it. Her cheeks were slightly reddened and the wisp of fair hair on her left temple looked like down.

"I'll never leave you alone with her again," Jeff replied jokingly, but deep down he agreed Tom was right.

As the years passed, they would sometimes take Alice even to *The Den*—Eva was initially against the idea, but then Skippy brought her in to inspect it (having first spent the whole day tidying up) and, after some hesitation, she agreed. Of course they didn't always find time to clear up before Alice's arrival, but she actually enjoyed being among all those empty bottles, beer cans and the tottering piles of old newspapers and magazines.

"We're a sort of attraction for her, don't you see?" Tom assured Jeff. "Her mum's tidy flat is boringly commercial, whereas this here is *counter-culture*. In her eyes, *The Den* is something like *alternative family living*."

"Did you love my mum as well?" Alice asked Tom one day.

She glanced at Skippy, took the edge of her T-shirt between thumb and forefinger and hooked it over her front teeth. Tom pretended not to have heard. Alice tapped him on the shoulder.

"Did you love my mum, or not?" she slurred.

"Of course. You know my liking for monsters."

Alice laughed, but she wasn't to be put off.

"No, really, tell me," she insisted. "Did you love her?"

Tom turned to face her:

"Yes, I did. She was... unbelievably beautiful. She *is* unbelievably beautiful."

Alice nodded.

"But she was going out with Jeff," Tom explained. "It happens."

Alice lapsed into thought. She had a big wet patch on her T-shirt.

"So actually you all loved her," she laughed. "All three of you."

"Not Skippy, I don't think," Jeff remarked matter-of-factly.

Skippy looked ill at ease.

"I believe," said Tom, "that Skippy loved her as well."

"It's obvious he did!" said Alice flatly with a glance towards her father. "Otherwise he wouldn't keep coming to see us, would he?"

This was news to Jeff—and to Tom, as he instantly saw from his expression. No one said anything. Alice's eyes roved the room, ending with Skippy.

"Oops, *sorry*," she apologised. "I've blown something, haven't I?"

Tom was the first to twig:

"Wednesdays? Does he visit on Wednesdays?"

Alice nodded slowly. Skippy blushed.

"So no Jágr's Bar?" said Tom. "So no big screen? No blokes and beer on tap and a great atmosphere?"

"I only watch the football!" Skippy cried.

"On a fifty-five inch screen?" Jeff asked.

Skippy clasped his hands together.

"What are you thinking?" he said, his voice rising. "You're stupid! You're just being stupid!"

Jeff and Tom both watched him in silence. Skippy fell to his knees.

"I swear by the life and good health of all those near and dear to me that it's true! We watch football! That's all! All right?"

The scene was distinctly awkward, but convincing enough for all that. Tom's smile returned.

"Maybe you don't know, Skippy, but Eva was bagsied by Jeff here," he said in a belated attempt at a joke.

"What do you mean, *bagsied*?" Alice was quick to ask.

If there's something you don't understand, don't ask, Jeff thought.

TOADY

My husband Boris is a station supervisor on the metro. His mission in life is to keep advising travellers that the train approaching will terminate at Kačerov. After all my girlhood dreams of a rich, successful husband who would every day blow me a kiss as he left for work (our three adorable children and I would be standing on the glass-fronted terrace of a Functionalist suburban villa), I've wound up in a tower block on an estate, living with a man who spends eight hours a day hectoring people for crossing the yellow line along the platform edge.

As I travel around visiting the successful people whose apartments I furnish, I can't avoid the station where Boris works, so I at least try to stand where he can't see me from his post. I usually spend the wait scrutinising the pretty girls and trying to guess what they'll be like in ten or twenty years' time—basically it's analogous to doing a computer simulation of an interior (I'm sure that not one of those young women confidently boarding the train would dream that she might discern, inside the head of this dumpy, ill-kempt, oldish brunette, a fairly true image of her future self). Of course I'm permanently on the alert—so if one day there's a sudden crackle in the station loudspeakers, I may well be the only person to register it.

"Passengers travelling towards Háje are requested not to cross the yellow line," came my husband's voice, altered almost beyond recognition by having constantly to repeat the same old thing.

I stared down at the grey marble of the platform.

"Passengers travelling towards Háje are requested *not to cross* the yellow line!"

In this second announcement even someone who didn't know my husband could have detected fatigue and resignation. The stout man at whom the admonition was directed remained leaning out over the rails, clearly taken by something down on the trackbed. I took in his apparel and it was instantly clear to me, if not to my husband, that he was foreign. The train approaching could already be heard in the tunnel.

"Get behind the yellow line!" Boris shouted into the microphone, now clearly rattled, but in the end he had to come running out of course—thin, pale-featured, in that shapeless brown uniform—and pull the chap back by his sleeve. The foreigner was startled, but as soon as he understood the situation he launched into an exaggerated apology. My husband doesn't speak any foreign language; he put on an act of ill temper and made to leave, but the fat man started patting him on the back and even tried to give him a friendly hug. The train came in and the alighting passengers checked out the funny-looking pair. I quickly boarded the train and the doors began to close. I had a last glimpse of Boris smiling awkwardly—and I had to bite my bottom lip so as not to burst into tears. It works just as well as when I pinch my hand.

I've had years of practice at both.

I love a metro station supervisor—and I have this constant need to explain it. It's odd: of course I know in theory that life is unimaginably diverse, multilayered and resistant to any kind of simplistic account of it, and so on, but whenever I run up against even the slightest actual hint of the *genuine* variety of life, it usually catches me out. A black man is walking along Kaprová Street with a randypole at Easter time and I gawp at him like at an apparition. But there's no need for any such extreme example: even today

I am amazed that my husband Boris can be *at once* kind-hearted and xenophobic, sensitive and *at the same time* obtuse. One time he's soft and tender—and another time he acts like a textbook boor (so not remotely fit for purpose as a character in a soap opera).

I'm immodest enough to suggest that much of the better side of Boris is down to me. Plenty of his friends to this day remark approvingly that Boris has much improved in my (corpulent) company. I met him in 1991 on a two-day coach trip to Venice (at the time Dad had started driving a new double-decker Neoplan, which he never stopped going on about, so I signed up for the trip myself); Boris was travelling alone. I liked his docile appearance and the slight greying around his temples; he also wore *white* sandals—if he hadn't had terry-cloth socks with the wonky inscription SPORT on both ankles peeking out of them and if there hadn't been that large leatherette bum bag containing his documents and bobbing about above the flies of his cheap denim shorts, I might have taken him for a doctor (doctors, with the obvious exception of Skippy, are second only to toreadors on my personal scale of the erotic; I've no idea why—it could be that I subconsciously associate doctors with safe, in some way *disinfected* sex, except how, in that case, could I account for all those sweaty and doubtless promiscuous toreadors?).

Boris sat right at the front, often leaning forward slightly and watching Dad's driving; whenever Dad gave vent to his annoyance at some *Italian cretin* who was trying to sneak in ahead of us, Boris would nod in approval. Only then would Dad beep at the car in front—I had a secret suspicion that he only wanted to hear the loud, hearty sound of the horn—

followed by a hand with the middle finger raised shooting out of the window of the black Golf.

"Iti prick!" Dad would unburden himself.

Our relief driver was still asleep, so having first sought me out in his rear-view mirror and finding no moral support, he glanced briefly at Boris.

"Where's that idiot think he's going in such a hurry?" Boris said ingratiatingly.

During a break at a motorway service area they exchanged a few words. From the on-board coffee machine Dad was selling drinks to the passengers while I, with an ironic, almost apologetic smile (which was a total mystery to most of them), handed out the plastic spoons, milk and sugar. Boris kept flapping around nearby: he clearly didn't understand my position, but he was also afraid to ask. Back then, his self-assurance was of a low order: if someone took his seat in the cinema, he'd rather go and find another; if it was packed out, he'd sit on the steps. When dealing with shop girls under the age of thirty he would always develop a stammer. And so on. He'd had a couple of relationships of some duration, but the amount of time he'd spent alone with his complexes exceeded them by far. Who else but I could understand him better?

On the return journey he and Dad kept up a lively conversation. My father—wonders will never cease—even laughed out loud, and more than once.

"I see you've got a new pal," I told him during the next *toilet break* with a light toss of my head in the direction of Boris. My father looked blank. He walked round the coach carrying a bucket and using a wet brush to remove the dead insects from the headlights. I trotted obediently along behind him.

"Or have you developed something deeper between you?"

Father set down the bucket and made a gesture of clipping me behind the ear (he can't abide homosexuals and invariably refers to them as queers). Then he told me where Boris worked.

"I see," I said, smiling, "you get on so well because of a shared belief that all passengers are beasts, is that it?"

"We haven't got round to passengers yet," Dad replied primly. "Though it's likely we'd agree on that point too."

"*Too*? What *other* points do you agree on?"

Finally he looked straight at me.

"I reckon he's a decent bloke," he said aggressively.

We looked hard at each other.

"Dad, stop right there!" I warned him.

"At least it'd be *something*," he went on with a frankness that shocked me.

That 'something' meant he knew about my *nothing*.

"Now I'm wondering if I shouldn't hitchhike the rest of the way," I said.

At journey's end, and to Dad's great delight, Boris and I introduced ourselves. Boris asked with a stutter if I often travelled with my dad.

"Only when they give him a Neoplan," I joked. "I wouldn't be seen dead in a Karosa."

Dad laughed. Boris roused himself for a direct question:

"And when's your next trip with a Neoplan, Zdeněk?"

I was gobsmacked: they were already on first-name terms!

"Next weekend. Two days, Vienna–Mikulov. Are you coming?" he asked, turning to me.

I looked daggers at him.

"I don't know."

"I'd come," said Boris.

In a wine cellar in Mikulov, Boris and I also switched to first names.

As an opener, and for want of other options, I began with Irena's suicide; I was surprised to discover that Boris knew all the details. Yes, a colleague of his had actually spotted her. For a while she'd been seen running up and down the edge of the platform, but not the wrong side of the yellow line, so he hadn't intervened. Allegedly she even kept bumping into people.

"And didn't he find it a bit odd? Why didn't he act?"

"He were new," said Boris. "Barely a week in the job."

"Right."

"And 'ave you any idea 'ow many different kinds o' nutters we get in a day?"

This lack of tact was offensive. Irena hadn't been a *nutter*, I retorted mentally. She was just an unhappy, very plain young girl whose life had been a living hell.

Back home, and surprisingly unharmed, we survived the inevitable embarrassment called our *first real date.* After the second, unexpectedly pleasant one I started getting a bit edgy. So far a good-bye kiss was all there'd been, but what might come in a week's time? Obviously I couldn't tell Boris I was a virgin (though thanks to my *technical prowess* with auto-erotic fun and games I wouldn't have to). A virgin at twenty-nine, that's just not normal, it would frighten him off—in his eyes I'd instantly turn into goods that no one bought.

So from the muddy bottom of the lock at Střelecký Island I had to dredge up Libor: I washed him down, dried him off and got him walking again. As recently as a few days before he'd been a bloated green corpse, and now he was smiling at me again. He was smoking again and tapping the ash into the palm of his hand. I relearned all the requisite background—with distaste and a degree of sentimentality, like when an actor rehearses a long forgotten part. Yet all of a sudden, a single lover by the age of twenty-nine started to look a bit thin. I mustn't underrate myself, I thought, hell, I must have greater faith in myself. Why, by twenty-nine, couldn't I have had at least *two* lovers?—And who needs to keep inventing blokes? I answered my own question. Who's to keep remembering everything? I fumed, but then I had a bright idea: I'd bring onto the field Petr Stančev, a happily married colleague at work. I knew plenty about him so—sex apart—I didn't have to fib. I was a woman trying to convince her partner that she'd once had *something going* with someone at work.

"And why did the thing with Stančev actually come to an end?" Boris was curious to know later.

"I got sick of all his false promises," I explained.

After Boris and I had first made love, he asked me shyly if the two previous ones had been *a lot better?*

"You're trying to compare what can't be compared," I said with conscious ambiguity.

"What does that mean," he asked in a strangled voice.

Good God! Men!

"Petr was always in a hurry to get home—if you get me? Wham, bang and home to Mam."

Boris smiled.

"Before I realised we were onto something it was all over."

For a while he just stroked me gratefully, but then it had to come.

"And Libor?"

"He was like a little kid," I said with tender disdain. "He looked like a little boy."

I leant over to Boris.

"Do you need to know what little boys look like?" I whispered.

He shook his head, but I wasn't deceived. He didn't need to know, he wanted to hear.

"I couldn't even feel him inside me," I said, *bashfully* covering my face.

So I wasn't actually lying this time either.

SKIPPY

My so-called father abandoned my mother when I was only five. It has to be said, though, that too much can be made of these things; in my own case, a few years passed and I stopped thinking about him. Now he's got diabetes and has lost two toes because of it. I can't say I'm particular bothered, but Mum always sends him a pretty conventional Christmas card, so I sign that at least. The idyll of Christmas, tee-hee. Mum lives with a partner of sorts. And he's an odd sort at that. For example, he had the bright idea of pooling their pensions, keeping them in an empty Mon Chéri chocolate box. Which they do—then he takes all the money and graciously gives my almost seventy-year-old mum a weekly allowance. A real sweetie, he is: when he first learnt I was a gynaecologist, he started flicking his tongue in and out and giving meaningful winks. I reckoned it was only a matter of time before he asked to borrow a white coat and come with me for a day out. Before going round there for an obligatory lunch once a month I dose up on anti-nausea pills (metaphorically speaking). Mum can clearly tell he's an idiot, but she probably thinks it's better to suffer an idiot than loneliness. On the one hand that's understandable. When Tom went and married his fairy princess and Jeff hadn't got divorced yet, my own loneliness in *The Den* got so bad that I'd talk back at TV anchormen. It got quite serious. For the first time in my life I went to investigate a queer bar, but turned back on the third step. I knew at once I didn't belong there. For one thing, I've always been a bit of a loner, but above all it's probably that I'm more asexual than homosexual. Given that I'm still a virgin at forty-one, that probably doesn't surprise you. Would I even have known how to talk to full-time poofs? Are you into arm-stroking? Can I put my head on your shoulder, is it okay? Fortunately, both Jeff and Tom got divorced quickly enough to spare me the trouble of trading a shag for a chat. I threw a welcome party for them in *The Den* and everything was back like in the good old days. It soothes me to hear them taking a shower or clattering about in the kitchen. Even today, at breakfast, Jeff can still look like Michelangelo's *David* stirring his coffee. More than that I can't have: *Shto dyelat?*, as our Russian teacher used to say. So: Early in the morning the maiden gets up, stroking her fanny as she downs her first cup. I know there are more dignified ways of coping, but since they've got me pigeon-holed the way they have, why go complicating matters? You can't teach an old dog new tricks. No one can change the image others have formed of us. And anyway, it's quite enough for me that Jeff takes me away with him and Alice at the weekend—those are almost happy times. We function as a normal, decent family, so who cares what the conservatives of this world might think? In a nutshell, those weekends are the nicest thing that's ever happened to me. Does that strike you as a bit thin? Then what should Karel, Ruda or Irena say? Where does it say that every mushroom-picker has to come back with his basket full? Like it says in holy writ, morning's best for doing it. For God's sake, Skippy, shut it. Tee-hee.

TOADY

In a sense, the wedding was my magnum opus.

But then I'd always believed that, if I put my mind to it, I could actually achieve, if temporarily, a certain allure, given the right *window-dressing*—and the wedding fortunately confirmed this suspicion. With the aid of half a pound of make-up, blusher, lipstick, mascara, eye-liner, whitening tooth-paste, a dose of laser treatment, a push-up bra, a bodice, a cream-coloured wedding dress from Paris (with two discreet little gussets) and a simple bouquet of tea roses I created something akin to a sand cathedral. So there you have it, I complimented myself in front of the mirror (Dad was standing behind me, almost suffocating with joy), all it takes is a hairdresser, a beautician, a dermatologist, two seamstresses and a florist—and for a few hours I'm not plain. Between our arrival at Nusle town hall and the lunch at Banseths' opposite I was, *after a fashion*, beautiful. The girls from my class at school scrutinised me with suspicion, while the boys were puzzled as to why they'd never actually shagged me.

At least I hope they were.

At my request, Boris was wearing tails, which left him rather ill at ease—and when Stančev, my colleague from work, gave me a long kiss on the lips after the ceremony (I can't think what had got into him), he got even edgier.

Tom just gave me a sloppy kiss on the cheek.

"Hm, that time at Slapy you did it a lot better," I reproved him.

"Can I touch you?" Marie asked Boris and she laid a hand on his arm. "How very odd. You're real..."

Then she gave me a hug.

"Sorry, sorry, sorry," she whispered.

When it came to his toast to the newlyweds, Dad made quite a drama of how he'd brought me up, all on his own.

"When she was three months old," he said, pointing at me, "her mother deserted us. Just upped in the night and left. All she left me with was some baby formula and a feeding bottle."

I prayed he'd cut out the bit about her stealing his radio. Fortunately he went on to how he bought me my first glasses.

"She must have been about eight," he said. "They were those cheap national health specs for kids. When she put them on, it tore my heart out. Not to put too fine a point on it, they didn't do her any favours."

Some of the guests, who wrongly supposed this was a joke, laughed. Dad put them down with his customary bus-driverly scowl.

"In short, seeing her in those little specs made me realise how terribly vulnerable she was."

He got a lump in his throat and couldn't go on. I dug a nail into the skin beneath my thumb and took the deepest breath possible.

"Daddy?" I cried. "This is a wedding, dammit!" It's supposed to be a *joyful* event!"

The relief in the guests' laughter was quite audible.

"I only meant to say we didn't have an easy time of it... But we did cope in the end."

"To the bride and groom!" yelped Skippy amid the applause. "And skirts up!"

Three hours later, I took that fabulous dress off, washed the only face fit for purpose that I'd ever had down the plughole and metamorphosed back into plain old Toady.

THE AUTHOR

In December, two months before I was to submit the manuscript to the publishers, Grandma K. came to spend a few days in Sázava. The following year she'd be ninety, though she still enjoyed relatively good health, a fantastic memory and a sharp mind.

After lunch, the author took her out for a longish walk; the paths were icy, but Grandma had a bit of wood that she used as a stick, and they were holding hands anyway. She rattled on and on in her customary monotone; the author only began to pay more attention when she voiced aloud her regret at having lost contact with some girl in her class at high school.

"How many of you were there? In class, I mean," he asked.

We were talking about the Girls' Reformed High School in Silesia Street in Vinohrady, where she'd been a pupil from 1929 to 1933.

"Twenty-nine."

The author pondered how to ask tactfully about the here and now. Grandma made it easy for him.

"There are only three of us left," she said.

Dodgeball—the first thing that occurred to him.

"Manka, me and the one I've no address for," she went on calmly. "Though she's probably dead now as well."

"You used to meet up quite often, didn't you?" said the author after a pause.

"Yes, but only after the war. Before the war not so often. After the war there were only twenty-one of us. Eight hadn't come through it."

The author asked about the circumstances: two had died in a concentration camp (one a Jew, the other a communist), two of typhus and one of TB. Grandma listed them all by name. She had no idea how the other three had died.

"So how often did you meet?"

"Once a month, if you please!" Grandma announced with pride. "Always at the home of one or other of us. The hostess would always cook and bake loads of food. Sometimes it was a real banquet! This stick's annoying me."

"All right, let's dump it somewhere."

Grandma wasn't going to wait and dropped it right there on the snow-covered pavement. The author had to laugh.

"The very first post-war reunion was one I organised! There were eighteen of us! Eighteen out of twenty-one!"

"That's good."

"You're telling me. Two sent an apology, but not the third. She really made us mad. When we asked her why she hadn't come, she said: *And what good would it have done me*? Tell me, wouldn't it have made you mad?"

"It would," the author agreed.

TOADY

The trees in the hospital grounds have lost most of their leaves and through their bare branches you can see buildings that only a few weeks back were invisible. The dead leaves have gone dry and hard and with every puff of the cold November wind they make an almost rasping sound on the asphalt; in many places all that's left of them is a brown pulp, but under the cherry trees next to the pavilion where Dad's ward is, the last rich colours are still showing: a warm yellow and crimson. I clutch at them with my eyes like a drowning man clutches at a straw.

"Dad? Do you want a drink?"

I repeat the question several times over, but the only response comes, as usual, from the old boy in the next bed; today he keeps shouting something like *lizard*. I know he wants me to answer.

"Yes, lizard. An amphibian," I said without batting an eyelid; I'm quite practised at such pseudo-dialogues.

"Blizzard!" he manages to scream. "Blizzard!"

"All right. Blizzard. Or gizzard," I say the first thing that comes into my head and he surprises me by falling silent.

He's an alcoholic in *the final stage* (when the nurse told me that, I did wonder what stage Tom might be in).

Dad has completely stopped talking, though his eyes are open. It frightens me. What on earth's he seeing? I wonder. What's he thinking about? I pat his hand and offer the dummy of his drinking bottle up to his sunken, stubble-encircled mouth. He doesn't respond; so I tip the bottle up a bit and he can feel the first drops and now his cracked lips move ever so slightly and he starts to suck. Forty years ago this was how he used to feed me.

There'd been times in the past when I was glad of his silence—like the time when Irena was staying with us.

I could tell what mood he was in from the way he unlocked the door and how he tossed his keys down on the shelf by the door (the black formica still shows the marks and is chipped here and there).

"Hi, Dad."

"Good afternoon," said Irena.

"Afternoon," he grunted.

He took off his shoes (in later years, having come in from work, he would sit down in the hall on the shoe cupboard), wheezing, he put his shoes away and, with complete disregard for Irena's presence, he took off his blue work trousers. I wondered if he'd have gone about in his boxers just as blithely in the presence of Eva Šálková.

"Bad day, Dad?"

"People are bloody animals."

I glanced at Irena and shrugged apologetically. Dad folded his trousers carefully and I put them on a hanger for him.

"All people?"

Irena wore an uncertain smile. Dad dismissed my irony with a wave of his hand, took from the shelf the copy of

Rudé právo that I'd taken from the letter box earlier that afternoon and went through to the kitchen to light up.

Until November 1989 he'd been almost a law unto himself inside his bus: under the Communists people didn't argue much with uniforms (even a bus driver's).

"You 'ave to give it to the Communists in one thing at least: people 'ad more discipline," he used to say after the revolution.

But even back then people could still drive him spare: they'd get on the bus with dogs unmuzzled, they'd open the roof window without asking him first, or they'd refuse to budge when asked to move on down. And so forth. I'd seen scores of such conflicts: *Either you get off the bus this instant an' take that unmuzzled dog with you, or the journey ends right here.* Guess who won.

"If they want to use the bus, they 'ave to take notice. If they don't wanna take notice, they can get 'emselves a Lada."

There was a malevolent superiority in his voice: he knew very well that most of his passengers couldn't afford a car. He had them over a barrel.

After the November revolution things started to change. Discipline went right downhill. People got more and more insolent.

"You can 'ave too much of a good thing," he told me once. "Even that damn' freedom of yours!"

I hadn't talked politics with him for ages, but this was a bit thick.

"*My* freedom? For goodness' sake, it's your freedom as well, isn't it?"

"Not a freedom I partic'ly care for."

Soon everything became clear: he'd just been through the worst incident of his career. He'd *flayed* some guy for boarding the bus with an ice cream cornet in his hand; the guy hadn't batted an eyelid, unhurriedly finished his ice cream—and then he'd grabbed Dad by the throat and torn his company tie off.

"Don't go getting ideas above yourself," he bellowed at him. "You're not the parish priest, asshole! You're a soddin' bus-driver, geddit? The only thing you're good for is drivin' the bus. So cut the preachin' an' drive, damn you!"

Dad had been left in shock. He could scarcely keep the bus on the road. He'd never been so humiliated in his entire life. Even as he told me about it he was shaking all over. Under the Communists nothing of the kind had ever befallen him.

In later years he'd voted for the People's Party. It took some effort on my part to squeeze it out of him, but when he finally confessed, unwillingly, I had to catch my breath.

"The *People's Party*, Dad? Am I hearing right?"

Sládek's Republicans would probably have come as less of a surprise.

"Explain yourself: why would someone like you opt for a Christian party?"

Dad frowned; he was finding the subject unsavoury.

"Tell me, Dad. Why? Has God ever made anything easy for you? Has He ever helped you in any way at all?"

He stared at me.

"That's my business an' mine alone. Anyone else can keep their noses out."

That was about as much as I ever got out of him.

Even last week he was still talking.

"Get something done about the flat, will you! I keep telling you..."

With an irritated wave of his hand he flapped away my assumed ineptitude.

"I will, Dad."

"You've got money, so where's the hold-up?"

Not even I know. We'd been talking about a total renovation for years, but never got beyond the planning stage. At the various furniture showrooms they've taken to laughing at me. A case of the blacksmith's horse. I invariably pick up their latest catalogue and then fail to get back to them for the next twelve months. If they phone, I tell them the truth—I'm still hesitating. An interior designer hesitating over a very ordinary, threadbare, burgundy carpet, a monstrous set of mahogany wall units and a three-piece suite that looks like a pile of sausages... Two years back I'd given Petr at work a whole carton of Spanish red with the request that he do me a few sketches—I made out that it was too close to home for me to do it myself and that I'd be incapable of rational thinking.

"Some doctors also don't like operating on relatives..."

He'd asked if I wasn't being over-sensitive; I told him I fully shared his fear.

"Get yerself some dodgy Italian bed and a glass table," Dad said. "Try Danish..."

Beneath the white bristles of his moustache I could see what might just pass for a grin.

"I will, Dad."

Tears forced their way into my eyes and I had to look away. A nurse spotted I was in trouble and came to my aid.

"Glass table," Dad said shaking his head disparagingly. "'Ave you ever 'eard such nonsense?"

"Before I die, you mus' come an' see me every day," he told me on Sunday.

He was having problems with his diction. Of course I made out he wasn't going to die—what else can you do? I should have said: 'Yes, Daddy, you're going to die very soon. In no time at all you'll have lost everything: body, appetite, memories, light, warmth, me...' Why don't they teach us these things? Why on earth do we keep studying integrals, protozoa, anorganic compounds and other such nonsense when—unlike dying—we don't need them in life? If instead of protozoa we could swot up on the rules of dying, at least that would be of some use.

Now Dad's dropping off again.

"Make way!" the old man in the next bed shouts impatiently. "Make way!"

"Hemingway," I replied reassuringly. "I was reading him only yesterday."

This time, too, he quietened down again. At least that afforded me some satisfaction.

EVA

Each year she quite looked forward to the class reunions that Marie and Zuzana continued to organise with such remarkable perseverance—in fact more than she could herself understand. 'Why do I do it, what's in it for me?' Eva would ask herself, yet she invariably went to the hairdresser's and got herself something new to wear.

Latterly, the numbers attending had risen again. Probably a product of sentimentalism. As Tom put it: *nostalgia will clutch at anything*. He believed they'd begun to realise there was no other, better youth waiting for them, so they were trying to make the best of the one they'd actually had. Another asset of reunions was their very *predictability*: the world was changing so fast as to be frightening, while at reunions they might occasionally surprise, but not frighten, one another. They knew what to expect of one another. He just might have been right.

The first year after their divorce Eva and Jeff both showed up, from spite. It's just as much my class as yours, her eyes told him. Jeff, closely watched by the others, gave her a quick peck on the cheek. They sat apart, obviously. She could tell he was up for a good time, but that her being there put a damper on it. He also kept track of whoever went and sat with her, such as Skippy or Tom. In the end he could take it no longer; he got well and truly drunk and started snogging, for all to see, a total stranger, a girl he'd met on the way to the toilet—and he did so looking Eva straight in the eye. Thereafter she and Jeff took turns: she came in odd years, he in even.

In the year in question it was Eva's turn.

She got off the tram one stop early and deliberately took her time, yet she still got to the restaurant first. For over twenty minutes she sat alone at the only vacant table and kept having to deflect the hoards of new arrivals.

Four bright young faces; one—a girl's—broke away and headed towards her.

"Sorry, this table's taken," Eva repeated patiently. "We've got a high school class reunion."

A disgruntled, disapproving pout. They'd come to have a good time and this old bag was being difficult. 'Have we lost the right to life? I'm forty-one and she'd gladly hurl me off a cliff,' Eva ruminated angrily, while staring the girl out with an assertive smile on her face.

When Marie, Tom and the rest finally showed up, she told them all about it in reproachful terms.

"Next time, I'll aim to be at least an hour late! D'you know what it's like—sitting here for near on half an hour completely alone?"

"And facing the condescending gazes of those whose old age hasn't yet begun...," said Tom.

The others found the remark quite amusing.

"You find that funny?" Eva asked, mystified. "Do you find it funny having half of all TV commercials filled with skinny sixteen-year-old models? Is it normal?"

Later on, as they chatted about Prague's pubs and bars, she came up with the idea of having one called *Forty Plus*. She maintained that Prague urgently needed something of the kind. People of their age could dance there without the usual sense of impropriety.

"Mightn't Fifty Plus be even better?" Katka hazarded.

"There already is one," Marie noted, "except it's called Na Vlachovce."

She, Eva, was the only one not laughing, again. Maybe she genuinely lacked a sense of humour. She took in all those greyed fillings, bridges and crowns and wished she were dead. A waitress arrived and Tom ordered the wine.

"But just mineral water for me," Eva added.

Marie took three tea candles from her handbag and lit them one by one; the young folk watched with distaste from the adjacent table. Eva was thinking about Rudolf. He used to turn up at reunions in his car, although it had to be faster by tram or metro, and he'd have been saved the problem of parking, but he probably had his reasons; that was why he never drank, so together with Eva and a handful of other teetotallers they had for years made up a derided, discriminated minority. They pretended to suffer accordingly, but in fact they thought themselves a cut or two above all those *juiceheads*, as Rudolf used mockingly to call the others until two years previously, in the spring—and stone-cold sober—he died at the wheel of his new Opel somewhere up near the Polish border. *Come the morning and you'll be envying us, you juiceheads!* he used to say. 'What are they going to envy me for—the lack of a headache?' she suddenly found herself wondering.

And what next? Anything else?

"Oh all right, I'll also have a wine this time," she said to general amazement.

TOM

Each time our old classmates meet up, usually at the beginning, I have to tell the others about any changes that have come about at our old school during the intervening year; it's become almost a ritual. This year's reunion was no different.

"Well, come on, what's new?" Marie demanded to know without beating about the bush.

"I'm packing it in next year."

Silence reigned: they probably all realised that they'd be losing the last link to their high school days.

"Because of the money?"

Teachers' pay, the media cliché of the day. I may have doubted that my secondary school teacher's salary would feed the proverbial *family with kids*, but then I didn't have one—and the money I did get nearly always sufficed to cover the rent and the booze.

"No. I don't want to be working in the museum of my own youth any more—that's the main reason," I said and glanced at Eva, though the first to register her understanding was Toady.

I'd recently found myself setting the pupils written tests not only because it was a tried and tested method of getting a moment's relief from them, but also, and surprisingly, so that I could observe them undisturbed and set my mind to solving that monumental mystery: how was it that they were sitting at those very desks at which we'd sat only a few years before? I compared their young faces with the faces before me in the restaurant: our skin was obviously duller, our eyes deader, our teeth yellower and our hair thinner, but there's more to it than that. The face of a forty-year-old also begins to lose some of its symmetry: at eighteen its proportions are ideal (barring such cases as Irena Větvičková), while twenty years later you look either haggard or chubby. By the age of forty, what at eighteen had constituted a notable, interesting facial feature, such as wide cheekbones or a pointy nose, will often have burgeoned into something half-way to a caricature.

"And isn't it rather a pity?" Marie started to flatter me. "The pupils all like you..."

"Like?" Skippy repeated after her. "Don't they just! One of them liked him so much that she *married* him."

That was out of order. Skippy should have realised that our gradually ageing female classmates didn't want to hear tales of how their male counterparts had taken to marrying teenage girls.

"Tell me, how do you get pupils to like you?" Jiřina asked.

Her interest was sincere. She lived in a tiny village outside Prague with hardly any opportunities for this kind of discussion; it's almost fair to say that for her these reunions were something like supplementary training courses. Here she could ask questions that interested her and that it was beyond her bulldozer-driving husband to answer.

"I believe the main thing is to strike the right distance: to be neither too remote, nor too familiar. Poking fun at seventeen-year-olds when you're forty is embarrassing—as is getting all palsy-walsy with them. You have to find something in-between."

Jiřina was listening so intently as if she meant to become a teacher in the next life. A tram approached from Kinský Square.

"That is, if there even is any *in-between*," I added.

"Yeah, yeah, that was a great *in-between* with Klára," Skippy smirked and slapped me on the thigh. "*In between her legs*, I reckon!"

The bubble of embarrassment in which we were temporarily trapped was burst, surprisingly, by Eva.

"I'd say," she said sourly, "that you put that very nicely, *Doctor...*"

Our world-weary, greying and overweight class all laughed.

Later on the conversation went round in predictable circles: kids growing up, problems with flats, parents' ailments, our own ailments, treatments prescribed and unprescribed. The difference between youth and age: at forty, vaginal suppositories can be discussed aloud. Toady had recently lost her father, so there was a moment for shedding tears and staying serious for five minutes. The wine was good. I ordered two more bottles and then tried to imagine seeing our *gathering of has-beens* through the eyes of the young waitress. I poured myself another glass; as usual I was way ahead of the others—and as per tradition I tried to mask the fact with long quotations delivered impromptu.

"The distinction between children and adults, while probably useful for some purposes, is at bottom a specious one, I feel. There are only individual egos, crazy for love," I said with due pathos. "Donald Barthelme."

I was pleased to note that by this stage Eva and some of the other girls were also tipsy; over the course of the year their contact with alcohol would have been minimal, so they were easily overcome by just a few glasses. They smiled without speaking, lest their diction gave them away, and they were doubtless considering ordering another coffee.

"I've got a new jacket," I announced. "Bought it yesterday just for this evening. I wonder, did any of you notice?"

I was shouting slightly. Katka took the fabric between her fingers, rubbed it, then patted my arm without saying a word. Perhaps that's exactly what we *should* do at reunions, I thought: sit, drink and silently pat one another's arms. Wouldn't that be best? Zuzana spoke: struggling, she suggested we might go on somewhere for a dance. I felt for her: she'd never do anything of the kind on her own, so she was tempted by the chance of hiding behind the mass euphoria—or rather lunacy. Fortunately, I wasn't the only one aghast at the thought of us joining a bunch of teenagers at the nearest disco, so the suggestion was kicked into the long grass. Eva took her little jacket off; her cheeks were ablaze. She was still beautiful (one of those present had already compared her to the Lady of the Forest in *The Lord of the Rings...*), but the skin on her neck and chest had begun to loosen. A few wrinkles, a little fat—and so much sorrow. *When she came into my orchard / blossom time was nearly o'er.* Why do we teach this stuff to high school kids? I asked myself. How can they possibly grasp what the poet meant? Eva started tinkering with a candle and the wax trickled over her fingers.

"Where the hell did it all go?" I exclaimed, banging my fist on the table.

The surface of the wine in the glasses eddied. My former classmates exchanged embarrassed glances.

"I'll tell you this: usually the first sex isn't up to much, but the first *real* kiss..."

I tried to find the *mot juste*.

"It's *indescribable*. In my case, I thought I was going to completely *dissolve* in her."

Eva was smiling.

"The *savour*. Of course, today I know she must have been sucking some stupid sweet, but at the time I'd absolutely no idea. For years I thought, idiot that I am, that beautiful girls really do taste like strawberries."

I looked at Eva: provocatively, aggressively.

"Raspberries," she corrected me. "It was a *raspberry* bonbon."

"Nice one!" Skippy broke the silence.

"Well I never, the things we're finding out today," Zuzana said frostily.

"Where did it all go?" I went on. "If a girl kisses me today, at best I'll think: She's a good kisser. No more than that. Where did the total *paralysis* go? Where the sweet *stupefaction*?"

"Oh hell," said Honza, his eyes all a-twinkle. "Here he goes again, sozzled as a senator..."

I eyed him with something approaching hostility.

"Yep, I am. And what about it? Does that make it any less true?"

He looked taken aback.

"And what's Vartecký up to?" Eva asked unexpectedly.

She even looked me in the eye, but immediately averted her gaze (her momentary, almost *demure* daring reminded me of Klára). Most of us understood the historic significance of the moment: never before had she mentioned Vartecký aloud—after the raspberry bonbon this was now her second confession. My own feelings were mixed: in the first instant I was delighted by her openness, but at once I caught in her eyes a glint of that ancient passion, and it gripped my stomach just as it had back then. I was struck by an image of frozen raspberries: they have a white coating of frost, but something of their summer scent and flavour has been lost, though there's still enough there. The pot I'd just withdrawn from the deep-freeze of memory held the jealousy of twenty-five years past: it wasn't what it had been, but I fully recognised it for what it was.

"Vartecký?" I said, with as much indifference as I could muster. "Only yesterday we had lunch together in the *school dining hall.*"

"And? How's he looking?"

That was someone else asking, Eva had run out of courage. I pretended to be thinking.

"Do you remember that leather briefcase he had?"

My old classmates' faces lit up at once.

"He's still got it..."

"That's incredible!"

Eva was gazing somewhere into the past—as if that battered bag were some magical object that had brought Vartecký back to life.

"They really ought to give teachers a rise!" someone said with a laugh.

"What did you have?" Skippy asked.

"Beef in tomato sauce."

"And wasn't the meat a bit too tough for him? Are his teeth still up to it?"

The laughter grew louder. By now Eva was probably regretting that she'd asked. What had she hoped to get from it? I was sitting facing the window, so I was the first to spot the young couple staring in: the girl said something to her partner and pointed at us.

"But really, what is he doing now?" Katka said.

He used to go to the sauna in Podolí on a Friday—for example. But now he and his wife have bought a cheap cottage somewhere in Řevnice, on the flood plain, so—"

"How could anyone buy a cottage on a flood plain?"

"Think about it though," Zuzana responded, "if you're over sixty, like he is, the likelihood of experiencing a one-in-a-hundred-year flood must be lower, right? Then it's worth the risk. Do or die."

"Really? He's over sixty?" Katka was surprised to hear.

"What did you think?"

"Don't keep interrupting!"

"So," I pressed on, "he doesn't go to the sauna anymore, because on Fridays they now go off to the cottage. Which also explains why he scans the papers every day in the staff room and saves the advertising leaflets inside."

"Leaflets?"

"Advertising cordless drills, strimmers, disc grinders and the like. He compares the various offers. Baumax or OBI. The biggest battle of his declining years. On his office desk he's got—"

Eva rose with a clatter from the table. She lurched.

"Aren't you interested?" I asked her.

"No."

"But it was you who asked..."

"Except I wanted to hear... something nice."

"Well, I'm sorry," I said, throwing my arms wide, "but between *me* and Vartecký there's never been anything nice."

She closed her eyes and bit her lip.

"Tom!" Marie shouted at me. "Go easy!"

That brought me to my senses. I leaned aside so the waitress could take the empty glasses. Then I turned to Eva, but she'd gone.

"*Sorry.* I must be a bit touchy today."

"Christ," Toady chipped in, "to think you still live in that museum, after all."

EVA

Outside the ladies, where she'd gone for a good cry, she ran into a pretty blonde with a small tattoo on her shoulder, who looked her up and down with indifference. Eva estimated that one in four girls in Prague now had a tattoo, maybe as many as one in three. As she splashed water on her face, she envisaged what it would be like in 2050 when doctors' surgeries would be bursting at the seams with little old ladies sporting tattoos. The door opened: in the mirror she saw Tom's face.

"Come on in," said Eva. "There's nobody here."

"I want to apologise."

"Close the door. Close the door and kiss me."

She stepped closer and pressed up against him. Tom tried to resist.

"You'll be sorry in the morning," he said.

TOM

By midnight there were only nine of us left; I could have bet on it that they were all resolving not to come the following year. Eva asked me to call her a cab.

"Class reunions, mirrors of our wasted lives," I said.

"I call them contributions to popular entertainment," Toady laughed.

Then she instantly set about trying to work out the probable year of her death: if, she said, we took into account the average age at which Czech women die and factored in any family dispositions (*dispositions for dying*, I thought), it would be sometime in the 2030s.

"I've no idea why, but 2037 keeps nagging at me."

Whatever the case, the probability of her living beyond 2040, wasn't, she thought, very high; and to 2050 practically zero. It was actually quite simple. Toady's computations struck me as morbid, but she disagreed.

"They're the most natural calculations in the world. Everyone should realise that."

"I don't want to!" cried Zuzana with a shudder. "I'm young, beautiful and have my whole life before me—and woe betide the doubters!"

Changing the subject slightly, Toady told us about the feelings that assailed her as she dealt with some of her customers: specifically, a pair of ageing, endlessly quarrelling nouveaux riches who wanted her to fix them up with an apartment in which they'd be happy at last.

"Get it? Everything that for the last fifty years they've failed to get out of life, they now want to get out of furniture!"

By half past one, there were only three of us: Skippy, Toady and me. We were dead from fatigue and alcohol. Also dead were all the candles that Marie had lit at the start of the evening—I know she'd meant well, but either we were going to have a nice time, or sit at a table with three corpses; I didn't think the two could be combined. I looked at the empty aluminium holders. Dodgeball, I thought. The head waiter came to point out that they closed at one. Skippy was prepared to argue.

"Come on!" I ordered.

We scrabbled for our wallets and purses and counted and recounted the notes left by the others, but kept getting a different total.

"I never did like maths," Toady muttered.

I couldn't help myself, but she struck me as even uglier than usual. Skippy had another go at lining the money up in little piles.

"What's the point, screw it!" I said in exasperation. "Screw life. The wisdom of the future."

I waved and called to the waiter, who quickly counted the money—amazingly, he handed several 100-crown notes back.

"We can give 'em to Vartecký to cover any flood damage!" Skippy bawled.

"But he *hasn't been* flooded out yet," Toady objected.

"If he lives long enough, he will be. And if not, it can go to some orphans!"

The logic of inebriates.

"In which case you can give it to me," said Toady, struggling.

The waiter was smiling, out of uniform now. I scooped all the leftover money together in his direction. In one of my waves of lucidity, I managed to appreciate the fact that he still hadn't started treating us with disdain.

"Thank you. Do you know what Zweig wrote one month before his suicide?"

He shook his head.

"The life of our generation is now sealed. We no longer have the power to influence the tide of events, and we now have no right to offer advice to the next generation having been such failures in our own."

"Amen," said Toady.

Together we headed for Újezd, where Skippy threw up in the shrubbery at the foot of Petřín Gardens. Toady tried to convince me that we'd kissed during the post-exam party at Slapy. I know she used to love me, but had fortunately always had the good sense to keep it to herself. How many children had she got? One? Two? I can never remember things like that.

"And did we have sex? Was I any good?"

"Seriously. Just tell me: do you remember?"

"There's only one thing I remember: I was completely wasted. That's my traditional point of reference. The best aid for my memory."

Skippy was making ghastly noises. A little way off Zoubek's monument to the Victims of Communism stood glinting into the darkness: black human torsos. I pointed at them.

"That's us," I blurted in my folly. "Husák's children."

"Don't fool yourself, stupid," came Toady's stark response. "The tragedy in your life has got nothing to do with any regime."

When all's said and done she was right. Skippy rejoined us.

"Okay," I said. "Let's find some cosy all-nighter where we can pick over our lives' tragedies in peace."

THE AUTHOR

He hadn't marked New Year's Eve for years, the percentage of disastrous New Year celebrations during his lifetime having been so high that it couldn't be just coincidence. On New Year's Eve 2003 his scepticism had been reinforced by the fact that he'd had a quite unsettled year, most of which was spent on visits to the psychiatric hospitals and geriatric clinics where for many long months both his grandparents had been dying in tandem—though in the same period he'd had a daughter. Life giveth and taketh away... A cliché or a profound truth?

This time he was with his wife and daughter at Sázava; at midnight they went out onto the first-floor terrace to watch, at least from a distance, the town firework display. Veronika fetched a duvet from the bedroom and tossed it round their shoulders, and she brought the Phillips baby monitor as well. The brand brought back the Grundig paper anorak of his youth. He'd got over it, he realised. He'd survived.

"I've survived," he declared aloud. "Survived my own youth."

In part it had been to his own credit, in part a matter of luck. Not everyone succeeded: he used to meet others less fortunate in restaurants, on the street, at class reunions. He saw them on television, or read articles by them in the paper.

"Congratulations."

She was twenty-seven; she couldn't have understood.

On New Year's Day they took the pram to the river—for the first time in years it was frozen over. They walked for several kilometres over the snow-covered ice, meeting in all that time just two girl skaters with a dog.

"Do you know what you're going to call it yet?" Veronika asked.

"Dodgeball."

"You don't mean it's about the game, do you?" she asked in surprise.

"Sure, it's kinda like Stanislav Rudolf's *Fatty* for grown-ups."

"No, be serious. What's it about?"

As they walked, he pondered. He'd never actually asked the question himself.

"About people knocked out of the game. And those who made their way in life."

"And how many of those are there in the book? The ones who made their way?"

The author paused and started to count: he raised the thumb of his right hand—and hesitated.

TOADY

We didn't haul ourselves out of that ghastly all-night place until gone seven and it was eight before I got home. Boris was already making the children's cocoa in the microwave. I was reminded how the previous summer Dad had switched on not only the heating function, but the grill as well, so the plastic bowl I'd prepared his lunch in collapsed in the heat and the food got incinerated on the glass plate underneath. After that he only ever heated his meals on the gas cooker. He was equally against having a mobile phone. He wasn't cut out for the twenty-first century—as if those three years were just a follow-on from the century before. He made fun of airbags and ABS systems (not to mention headlights that follow the direction of travel at every turn of the steering wheel). His world was that of bus and trailer car, telephones with a circular dial, and his clunky, angular Grundig cassette radio. In his later years he reminded me of those old folk who some of my clients—led doubtless by the best of intentions—take with them to their new two-generation apartments and who then blunder about among all the minimalism staring in confusion at basin or bath and looking in vain for anything that might resemble a tap.

"Aha, here we are, home at last," said Boris playing at being a bit cross.

"And reeking like a tobacco factory."

The self-assurance that I'd once taken such pains to cultivate in him, like some delicate flower, he now used to effect against me. He would lecture me, criticise and tease me. Twelve years before he'd been scared of me, now he made fun of me. He had no hang-ups—any more than I had (I'd had to keep them hidden from him and the children for so long that I lost them; I know I still have some profound, fundamental self-doubt somewhere deep inside, but I've no need to go looking for it). And would you believe it, he would even flirt with other women in my presence? If I made some half-hearted protest, he would explain with ironic superiority just how things are in life. He let me in on those truths that I'd once revealed to him, and that he'd appropriated free of charge—no matter that I'd got most of them from listening to Tom. *To love does not mean to possess.*

He was unfaithful to me twice, but that entire year when Dad was dying he never set foot outside the house; he helped the kids with their homework, played with them, did the shopping, and the cooking, and he would sit up with me at night handing me paper hankies. I'd never have believed I could love someone who wore tweed hats, *hated* Vietnamese market stallholders and *adored* Helena Vondráčková—but it had happened. I gave him a hug.

"I love you, Boris. You know that, don't you?"

"There's the alcohol still talking," he said, smiling broadly.

Lukáš ran up, still in his pyjamas. I could tell he wanted to give me a kiss, so I bent down and offered a cheek. By contrast Andulka ignored me as she passed.

"Hi."

No response.

"What's the matter?" I asked.

Boris waited till Andulka had taken her cocoa and closed the door of the kids' room behind her.

"She thinks she looks *horrible*," he whispered.

Lukáš grinned gleefully.

"Never mind," I chirped, "she's got that from me."

TOM

Another lonely January weekend: Jeff had gone off skiing somewhere, and Skippy had flown to Australia for a month. I made myself a second spritzer. One part of me thought it a waste to add water to such a *good* wine, while the other part believed I really shouldn't be drinking it neat at ten in the morning. I idly finished the paper, including the two weekend supplements, then drew up a list of the people I could or should call. Of course in the end I phoned no one. I've always been surprised at how certain human attributes that ought to be mutually exclusive coexist quite successfully in reality: for instance, having an aversion to people and not being able to cope with loneliness. I poured myself a third, this time without the water. I despised myself, though my spirits did rise ever so slightly—even to the extent that I thought I might tidy the flat and so manufacture for myself some surrogate satisfaction, however flimsy. Tidying up—the methadone of alcoholics.

We used to assemble empty bottles first in the corner of the kitchen next to the waste bin and later, once they'd blocked access to the cooker, in the dark space behind the front door. We always bought beer in cans, because we couldn't have even more glass piling up, so it was definitely wine bottles that predominated; you might have spotted the odd Russian vodka label or one from a twelve-year-old Scotch that some woman had given Skippy in gratitude for cauterising her genital warts. My portion of the dust-laden bottles should theoretically have been one-third, but in reality I was the majority shareholder; that made me responsible for their removal. But just like any other job, I also tried to put this one off as long as possible, at least until the front door started banging into the bottles—that meant that every time Jeff or Skippy came in I got a kind of jangling reminder.

I got myself a sufficient number of plastic bags and started determinedly packing the bottles into them: the first, more numerous layer went in neck up, the second layer neck down. Some of them contained bits of precipitate, while only rarely did a few drops of wine go trickling down the plastic—in our household bottles got drunk dry. I ended up with nine bags; I took four in my left hand and five in my right and like a leper clinking his warning bell (and praying that none of the bags would burst) I left the flat and headed for the nearby bottle bank. In the street a taxi stopped and to my surprise Skippy got out: with a suitcase, in a crumpled summer suit and with a cowboy hat on his head. Even so, I was pleased to see him.

"Hi, Doc. You didn't stay long then."

He set his case down on the pavement, took hold of some of my bags and crossed with me to the green bottle bank. We each stepped up to one of the holes and starting feeding the bottles in.

"Big bang, eh, some bash!" Skippy shouted.

I wish.

A Note from the Translator

This is a book about nostalgia, consisting of the often less than fond recollections of a handful of one-time classmates who retell, often in the present tense in the original (preserved only sometimes in the translation, English being rather less tolerant of the device), individual events from their schooldays and from times twenty and more years later. They are a typically disparate bunch, each with their own recognisable discourse, but all are types that are instantly recognisable in any society.

This particular society is, however, the Czechoslovakia of the 1970s and the Czech Republic that eventually emerged in 1993 following the 'Velvet Revolution' of November 1989 and the dissolution of the Czechoslovak binary state with the 'velvet divorce'.

Every state and nation has its idiosyncrasies, some of which may not be familiar to outsiders. Hence this short note and the page-notes that follow. They come with an apology to those who are, conversely, entirely *au fait* with how Czech society developed in the decades following the so-called Prague Spring of 1968.

There are just three points I would make in this note:

1. The book's title: While the game of dodgeball is not unknown in the West, it has been hugely important in the context of Czech physical education, where it was played *ad nauseam*, apparently more loved by teachers than many of their primary and secondary school pupils. More important is its Czech name, *vybíjená*, which suggests 'knocking-out game', but it is derived from a verb, *vybít*, that has close associations with *zabít* 'to kill', can be synonymous with *vyvraždit*, and goes, *inter alia*, with the wholesale slaughter of diseased animals. It will not have escaped the reader how many of the characters, some *in absentia*, are 'knocked out' of society as in some sense oddballs, or die unhappily or are killed as the narrative unfolds.

2. Military service: On leaving school, young men had few ways of avoiding compulsory military service; at best it would be deferred for those who went to university first, after which they served for one year. Young men who did not go on to university had to serve two years. And as the book reveals, it was quite common for the population to be artificially mixed, by having young Czechs posted east to Slovakia and vice versa. Though the two environments had (have) much in common, there were (are) elements that can make the other place seem somewhat alien. The different, but largely mutually intelligible languages were probably the least of the problem.

3. Italics: In this novel, possibly more than in others by this author, italics are extremely common and will be seen to have at least four discernible uses: *a.* apparent and,

I believe, unwarranted imitation and extension of English usage, where it is normally used for emphasis only where word-order alone does not suffice (these cases are all preserved in the translation, despite their actual redundancy in places; they should be seen as a characteristic feature of the author's style); *b.* the translator's need to indicate that this or that phrase was in English in the source text; *c.* the translator's own English usage when, again, word order itself is insufficient to the requisite emphasis; and *d.* oblique citation and the citation of the names of works of art or literature.

The following page notes are intended to assist the reader over items with which some may be less familiar. Some items may appear redundant to the North-American reader, though not to the British reader, and vice versa.

p. 4 — *Complete Savages* is an American sitcom that was broadcast on ABC from September 2004 to June 2005.

p. 7 and later — *When she came into my orchard*: a quotation from a poem by Antonín Sova (1864-1928).

p. 27 — *Jágr's Bar*: The national sports of the Czech Republic are football and ice hockey, the latter always referred to as plain 'hockey', since field or grass hockey is hardly played at all, and is by some heartily despised! Perhaps the game's all-time greatest name is that of Jaromír Jágr (b. 1972), who played both in the national team and for numerous clubs in the NHL. One of the lesser features of the 'globalisation' of Czech society since the changes begun in 1989 has been the emergence of the 'sport bar', known perhaps more in the US than the UK, and one particularly swish one in Prague carries the name of this player. It gets several more mentions in the book.

p. 48 — *You passed through my dreams*: a genuine anthology of love poems by 36 Czech poets, compiled by Vladimír Karfík (original title: *Mým snem jsi prošla*, 1969).

p. 63 — Dan Bárta (b. 1969): a pop(ular) singer, known *inter al.* for singing with the Pilsen group *Alice* (Czech readers of the novel will have spotted the connection), but also for playing the water sprite in František Brabec's 2000 film of Karel Jaromír Erben's classic cycle of poems *Kytice* (The Garland), newly translated into English by Susan Reynolds (London: Jantar Publishing, 2013; the snatches quoted are given in that translation).

p. 78 — Tuzex hard-currency shop: Communist Czechoslovakia had two currencies: the non-convertible Czechoslovak crown and the Tuzex crown, for which foreign currencies could be exchanged and with which foreign goods could be bought in Tuzex shops. This obviously left plenty of scope for black-marketeering, hence the sleazy spivs hanging about outside; they would offer more than the going rate for any foreign hard currency carried by visitors to Tuzex.

p. 78 — 'waiting for a landline to be installed': at the period in question, the country was still battling to get landlines to everyone who wanted them. So having one was not something to be simply taken for granted.

p. 84 — *The Girl with the Lemon-yellow Scarf* (*Citronová holka*): a 1980s hit by the then heart-throb Vítězslav Vávra (b. 1953) which in time became a popular karaoke number.

p. 105 — Elán: a Slovak pop-rock band that was hugely popular throughout Czechoslovakia and remains so in both successor states. *Dancing Girls from Lúčnica (Tanečnice z Lúčnice)* is a particularly rousing number of theirs, also popular in karaoke.

p. 106 — *From the depths great waves...*: translation taken from Karel Jaromír Erben: *Kytice*, translated by Susan Reynolds (London: Jantar Publishing, 2013, p. 188).

p. 122 — Zadie Smith: The quotation is from early in Chapter 2 of her *White Teeth*.

p. 123 — "certain car-owners switch the badge on their car for another": this was quite a common practice as car-ownership became more widespread, for with it came the belief that a Western car was *eo ipso* better than any Czech car. Hence VWs and Fords lacking their badge became a common sight. To an extent, foreign car badges became collectors' items, which probably explains why, on a visit to the Czech Republic in the mid-1990s, my own Vauxhall, a rare breed on Czech soil, was deprived of its badge in a car park in broad daylight.

p. 137 — "randypole at Easter". One old Czech tradition that gets a brief mention here is what goes on at Eastertide: On Easter Monday it is the custom for boys and young men to go about with a plaited willow wand with ribbons on its end (it has an amazing range of regional names) and lash the calves and buttocks of girls with it. In return girls (who feign being offended if not so assaulted) give the boys painted Easter eggs. Older men may be rewarded with a shot of something alcoholic. Not much is made of the custom in the novel, and this note is merely to explain why the sight of a black man carrying such a willow wand, which I have called a 'randypole' is seen as incongruous (I got the term from the

London *Evening Standard* many years ago in a piece about Cornwall; I have never seen the expression since, but it seems very apt.)

p. 138–140 — *Neoplan*: a German manufacturer of coach and bus bodies, hence infinitely preferable to anything produced by the Czechoslovak *Karosa* company (cf. the preference for Ford over Škoda among car-owners).

p. 160 — Stanislav Rudolf's [b. 1932] *Fatty* (original title *Metráček* [Little Quintal]): a book about an obese teenage girl with an inferiority complex, also known from Josef Pinkava's 1971 film version.

David Short, Windsor, April 2018

ALSO AVAILABLE FROM PÁLAVA PUBLISHING

Irena Dousková
B. Proudew

Translated by Melvyn Clarke

Normalization? Collaboration?
The children are watching...

Irena Dousková
Onegin Was a Rusky

Translated by Melvyn Clarke

The loose trilogy carries on,
this time in Prague.

Martin Fahrner
The Invincible Seven

Translated by Andrew Oakland

Is it worth playing for the good guys?
This book has the power to convince sceptics...